DEMONS FIVE, EXORCISTS NOTHING

BY THE SAME AUTHOR

BOOKS

WHICH WAY TO MECCA, JACK?

JOHN GOLDFARB, PLEASE COME HOME

TWINKLE, TWINKLE, 'KILLER' KANE

I, BILLY SHAKESPEARE

THE EXORCIST

I'LL TELL THEM I REMEMBER YOU

THE NINTH CONFIGURATION

LEGION

SCREENPLAYS

THE MAN FROM THE DINER'S CLUB

JOHN GOLDFARB, PLEASE COME HOME

PROMISE HER ANYTHING

WHAT DID YOU DO IN THE WAR, DADDY?

A SHOT IN THE DARK

THE GREAT BANK ROBBERY

GUNN

DARLING LILI

THE EXORCIST

THE NINTH CONFIGURATION

THE EXORCIST III

DEMONS FIVE, EXORCISTS NOTHING

A Fable

WILLIAM PETER BLATTY

DONALD I. FINE BOOKS
New York

Donald I. Fine Books
Published by the Penguin Group
Penguin Books USA Inc., 375 Hudson Street,
New York, New York 10014, U.S.A.
Penguin Books Ltd, 27 Wrights Lane,
London W8 5TZ, England
Penguin Books Australia Ltd, Ringwood,
Victoria, Australia
Penguin Books Canada Ltd, 10 Alcorn Avenue,
Toronto, Ontario, Canada M4V 3B2
Penguin Books (N.Z.) Ltd, 182-190 Wairau Road,
Auckland 10, New Zealand

Penguin Books Ltd, Registered Offices:
Harmondsworth, Middlesex, England

Published in 1996 by Donald I. Fine Books,
an imprint of Penguin Books USA Inc.

1 3 5 7 9 10 8 6 4 2

ISBN: 1-55611-501-6
CIP data available

This book is printed on acid-free paper.
∞
Printed in the United States of America

For Julie, Peter and Paul

Part One

THE PSYCHIATRIST SPEAKS

Very Briefly

Did you hear that mysterious rapping, Siggie?
    —CARL JUNG, *Correspondence with Sigmund Freud*

TAPED MEMO TO FILE

May 20, 1994

THE FORTY-YEAR-OLD subject, Jason Hazard, a serious and highly acclaimed auteur on the American motion picture scene, presented today as acutely hostile, suicidal and paranoid with delusions, thus marking a major and welcome improvement over our previous appointment in which he completely denied my existence, a position he abandoned solely for the purpose of suggesting that I emulate *piblockto*, a bizarre and hysterical pathological outburst commonly seen among Eskimo women in which they dash madly about the igloo destroying the furnishings and decorations, and then run outside, rip off their clothes, throw chunks of ice at their pursuers and finally plunge into freezing waters. Seemingly reasoned, alert and well-focused, Hazard paints an anomalous and aggravating picture, interweaving real persons and actual events with fantasies, masks and delusional flights that are obviously camouflaged attacks upon myself: for example, his complaint of "DeMillephobia," a "paralyzing fear of talking to extras" which he sought to control, he doggedly insists, by attending a ten-day camp in Ojai set up by the Directors Guild for this purpose, not to mention his claim that we are in "Happydale," the asylum, if memory serves, in the comedy *Arsenic and Old Lace*, and not in my office on Central Park West. He appeared for his three o'clock session today in the regalia of a corporal of the Bengal Lancers, circa 1881, and brought me a gift, if one relies upon the label, of something called Mother Kali's Own Gin, with the further enticement and allurement underneath it: "A Favorite of Stranglers All Over Mother India." Clearly, this is more of his ferocious resistance in the guise of convincing me that he is ill and in the hope of prolonging these futile proceedings. My initial suspicion, therefore, remains—that Hazard is a man who has solved his problem but utterly loathes and detests the solution. However, this weekend I'll review our first session; maybe something's on the tapes that my notes have missed.

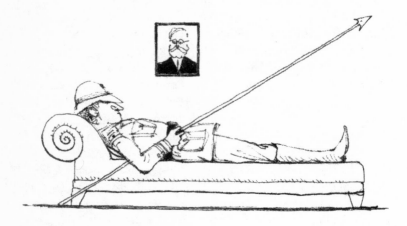

Part Two

THE PATIENT SPEAKS

THE FIRST TAPE

Some men need adversity to shape them; others respond to shapes adversely, especially in cases where the shapes are unseen.
—The Suppressed First Draft of Shakespeare's Hamlet

I'M A QUIET-SPOKEN MAN, a man of taste and modest judgments and not given to hyperbole or passion, but I want to state as clearly and as firmly as I can that my involvement with the seeming demonic possession of Barbra, my wife's Himalayan cat, and the subsequent and vivid attempts at exorcism by a legion of Jesuit priests, Warren Beatty and the Giant Rat of Sumatra, were all part of a mad fucking plot to destroy me, Doctor, a hideous and fiendish conspiracy which, as I recount it to your dumbfounded ears, will doubtless seem to you more tortured, labyrinthine and brazen than any one attempt at self-justification since Attila the Hun met Pope Leo I in the middle of a river and explained to him his concept of "eminent domain."

May I smoke? I hear you scribbling again: *"Paranoia."* Fair enough: that I once mistook Salvador Dali for a private eye could be true, I suppose, in some limited and esoteric technical sense, and is in any case a rumor that I'm tired of denying, though what Dali would be doing in the Russian Tea Room watching me intently in the midst of my divorce is a circumstance that *also* deserves to be mentioned. There are sometimes two sides to these stories.

Oh, God, I'm so tired. Where do I begin? The Big Bang? "Christ, we *made* that," Harry Cohn would have growled: "Lana Turner, Errol Flynn. I said bring me something *fresh!*" Good old Harry: at Columbia he put in a time clock—swear to God!—and the writers had to punch in and out, they had to prove that they were working from nine until five. One day the Epsteins—Phil and Julie, *Casablanca*—well, they turned in a screenplay that

Harry didn't like. "You *bestids*," he shrieked at the brothers, "this is *writing?* How the hell could you *wound* me like this, how could you *sheft* me when I've been like a *patron* to you boys, like a *father*, you esps, you goniffs, you stabbies in the beck!", raving endlessly on and on like this while spinning upward toward the ceiling in a cyclone of curses and making things somehow a Jewish *King Lear* until, finally, panting and frothing, he stopped, the huge whites of his eyes glaring up at the brothers like in one of his early zombie movies. "Mr. Cohn, I feel ashamed that the script is so rotten," Julie offered contritely, all earnest and abashed, and his kindly elf's face had this puzzled, lost look as he groped, "but I'm sure that I'm speaking for Phil here as well when I say that I really just can't understand it: check the cards—we were here from nine to five every day."

Harry's well-known creed was, "Give the people what they want!" When he died, they held the funeral service on a sound stage, stage Number Five on the old Gower lot. Groucho Marx leered around at the crowd in attendance, so many there was hardly air to breathe, the place was packed, and said, "You see— you give the people what they want and they'll turn out." There are eight million stories in the naked city, Doctor. Is that your red Rolls out in front? The Corniche with "ID DOC 1" on the license plate and the voodoo doll dangling from the mirror? I think you would have liked Harry Cohn, he was given to excess. On his deathbed he said "Rosebud" *twice.*

"Get to the part about Warren?" Nice. *Ta guele espece de connard*, you who sits there with all of the moral authority of a surreptitious fart, looking rapt and concerned while pretending to be listening and all the while anxious for this day to be done so at last you can hie yourself over to Sotheby's to bid on the garter belt worn by Freud and then fondle it nightly in that secret little room where you pen all those blackmail letters to your patients, the ones signed anonymously, "A Friend." This is *my* analysis, Doctor, *my* story, and I'll pace it as I please. Understand that? Good.

I first met Warren in the Egyptology Room of the British Museum in London where he was browsing while taking a break from his arduous study of the comparative incidence of "moveable nu" in the *Odyssey* and in Greenblatt's Delicatessen. Glancing up

coolly from the silent ponder of a curiously nonresponsive sar-
cophagus, he fixed me with squinty ice eyes as he softly inquired,
"You fuck my sister?", a theme which he would frequently come
to revisit as our friendship thickened on our march through the
woods and to which we may return for explanation later on, for
this is neither the time, I would think, nor the place.

"Is any of this true?" Are you utterly cracked, my liege? If I
knew what was fact from froth would I be here in this private little
laughing academy chatting it up with Norman Bates? Maybe it's
illusion versus reality. Yes. Did you ever see a movie called *Blow-
Up?* It's about a photographer who obsesses about what he sus-
pects is a murder in the park where he was doing a shoot a few
days before. He repeatedly enlarges a section of a photo where he
thinks he sees the murderer lurking in some foliage. The film was
a smash, I loved it, but some of the reviewers said there never was
a murder, that the theme was illusion versus reality. This made
me feel dumber than wheat. One night at Jim Bellows's house in
Brentwood I met the director of *Blow-Up* himself, the most pleasant Michelangelo Antonioni. "Was there really a murder?" I asked
him bluntly after shaking his hand and praising the film. He
looked at me oddly, and then answered, "Well, yes; I mean, at
least *I* thought so." I hauled out Life magazine's big clincher
about "illusion versus reality"—the scene at the end where some
revelers are playing an imaginary game of tennis with invisible
rackets, balls and net. "What about *that?*" I said; "what did it
mean?" Antonioni gave a diffident shrug and said, "Nothing. I
once saw some people doing that in Hyde Park and I just thought
it might turn out to be interesting footage."

Exactly. There is more to the eye than meets it. The truth is
I've never met Warren, I don't know him. I lied. I did it to get
your attention; Warren is "interesting footage," Warren's "hot."
Does that mean you're going to punish me again, Doctor Larry?
more shock treatment curiously focused on the anus without an-
aesthesia or a cigarette afterwards? Well, alright then, I have stag-
gering news to air out: yes, it's true that Warren Beatty didn't
figure in this story; but in fact it was someone even grander than
Warren: a giant, an immortal and legendary swordsman who
surely would have toppled every one of Warren's records were it

not for his startling and bizarre disappearance while alone on a private submarine ride at Disneyland: Yes, that's right, Doctor Larry—*Floyd God!*

Remember all the hullabaloo? The sub surfaced, but Floyd wasn't in it; they found only his clothing in a neat little pile, a list of the Rockettes in alphabetical order with all but the bottom two names checked off, and an unopened packet of "pre-owned" condoms that mysteriously vanished from the evidence locker, spawning rumors of a sinister murder conspiracy and tasteless allusions to "the smoking gun," even talk of a UFO abduction, which I daresay is the champion of mind-ebbing concepts: Floyd screwing his way through another whole planet? Never mind, he is dead and now a stamp but not forgotten. It was Floyd who helped me out with the Himalayan exorcism. Are you satisfied? *Now* may I smoke? That's alright, a non-filter would be fine, Herr Settembrini. Oh, how nice—I don't think I've seen a Domino since grade school. Your Grace, do you collect these or just pass them out to paranoids to help them feel they're probably on to something big?

I met Floyd through his sister, Sprightly God, who at the time was more celebrated than Floyd. I'd written a script or two that got made, and I somehow wound up in Sprightly's studio dressing room pitching an idea for a thriller with laughs. Sprightly was bankable; if she liked it, the film would get made. "How are you?" she said to me when we met. This of course was precedent to her days as a "channeler," or else she would have told me, "Good seeing you again," having known me from a previous life in Egypt when she was a pharaoh constructing the pyramids and I was a salesman from outer space selling anti-gravity devices to help with the lifting of "all those blocks." "Things really haven't changed all that much," she would have added with that waiflike pixie dimpled grin that made you want to immediately pick her up and unambiguously slip her the Constant Admirer while holding her aloft with both your hands so you could hear the steady clicks of the four-inch heels on her kiss-me-fuck-me shoes against the floor. Of course, I said nothing of this at the time. Instead, I was doing my Scheherazade act when the trailer door opened and Floyd stared in, looking somehow distracted and worried, yet inscrutable. When Sprightly introduced us, he nodded at me curtly, and then gravely and deliberately instructed Sprightly that if anyone identifying herself as either "Ramona or Trixie Montenegro" were to call to confirm that Floyd was really her brother, "Just be sure you tell her yes no matter *what* the hell she says." He then asked for the keys to Sprightly's new Jag so he could "take it for a spin" to the Springs "to buy dates." Accepting the jingling keys in silence, he threw me an unreadable, enigmatic look, and then quietly closed the trailer door and was gone. I finished my story, Sprightly liked it and in days we had a green light at Artery Studios, which happened to be run by Sprightly's husband, that ever-iridescent mad sonofabitch and destroyer of movies, Arthur Zelig. More of this amazing beauty later. Anyway, that's how I came to meet Floyd.

I saw him again at Sprightly's Christmas party. I found him to be bright and engaging and soon we were buddying around together; in fact, for six stupefying months we were roommates. On the eve of divorce, I'd packed a bag and left my wife in the wilds of the Valley. Correction—it was really my *wife* who packed the bag. Her problem, if you really must know, was jealousy, which is the feeling we tend to experience when someone we utterly loathe and detest is having a wonderful time without us. Never mind. In the meantime, Floyd had rented this house, a stately colonial mansion on Carrolwood Drive in Beverly Hills in advance of a visit by a young French actress, the gaminous and beautiful Lili Malraux, and I knocked on his door with my suitcase in hand looking miserable and happy and rich and broke and just asked him if he minded if I stayed with him awhile. Floyd didn't hesitate, he motioned me in. I was soaking; I had planned this for a stormy day.

The house had two wings, three pools and two tennis courts. Floyd kept a wing and gave the other one to me. That's the way Floyd was, spontaneous and generous. I hear your pissy silence, Doctor. That isn't what you wanted to hear? Very well—I was also the author of a script that Floyd wanted as a vehicle for Lili and himself and he wanted me under his eye and control until the deal had been made and the contracts signed; Floyd wasn't himself at this point, not God, just as I was not America's Ingmar Bergman yet, and he feared that I might sell out without insisting on approval of the film's director. But now listen to this, my idealist, my optimist, my Miranda of the Deeply Disturbed Ward: As it happened, Columbia wanted the script, which at the time was in something referred to as "turnaround," a term of art that is used when a studio decides to abandon a project and lets the author try to set it up somewhere else. Columbia'd agreed to Floyd and Lili as the leads but they craved a director that Floyd didn't like. Mike Frankovich, the head of the studio then, had invited me to come to his office for a meeting that had somehow been scheduled for eight P.M. when the building was certain to be otherwise empty. "Let's relax without the phones ringing," Mike had said gruffly. At the news, Floyd squinted and asked to come along. When I said, "What for?" he slouched away and shook his head, meantime breathily muttering in that leaf-rustling tone of his that makes half of what he says indecipherable; it could have been either "For luck" or "They have Kleenex."

When I entered his office Mike Frankovich exploded. "What the hell is Warren Beatty doing moosing around up and down the damn halls at this time of the night!"

"Warren Beatty?"

"Warren Beatty, Floyd God, what's the difference?" Mike bellowed. "Neither one of them was asked to this meeting!"

"Sir, he really isn't at it," I meekly evaded; "we're headed for Martoni's after this, he's just waiting."

"He's *lurking!*" the executive thundered.

This was true. In the silence of the building at that hour, you could hear Floyd's crepe-soled shoes squishing softly up and down along the carpeted studio corridors. Once I heard the water fountain running down the hall. Iron Mike tried to get me to focus on a deal, but I found I couldn't think. I was a nervous wreck.

"What happened?" Floyd asked me when the meeting was over.

I said, "Nothing."

Floyd grunted and might have said, "Good."

The next day I slipped away undetected from Manderley and returned for a meeting at Columbia, this time with a man that the studio had chosen to be the producer of the film; I had promised Mike Frankovich I would do this. The canny producer went straight for the groin. "I've got a contract right here on my desk," he smiled warmly; "if you'll give us the rights to the script right now, I've been authorized to write you a check immediately for eighty-five thousand dollars." He must have seen the blood drain away from my face because all of a sudden he was smiling like Iago in a Cosmo ad for silken handkerchiefs. He took a checkbook from a drawer and started writing. A million things occurred to me; one was an image of me grabbing the check and then running from the room without signing the agreement. The rest of the images were modeled on that one.

I said, "I can't do it." I heard my voice quaver.

The shithead looked up at me blandly, full of hubris, as he toyed with the poison-tipped platinum fang that Columbia issued to all its producers for purposes of honorable *hara-kiri* should one of their pictures fail to open. How did they know that Sony was coming?

"You can't?" the producer echoed, bemused.

I said, "No, sir, not unless it's written in blood that no TV director is assigned to this movie, most especially the one that Mike Frankovich mentioned as your absolute far and away first choice."

The producer's frozen stare was impenetrable; he looked like a stunned Sitting Bull after hearing from a scout that General Custer had snidely referred to him as "that spic."

"You have a problem with Roger Slime?" he questioned.

I told him, "With any TV director. I've promised Floyd and Lili that I wouldn't allow it."

For a moment the producer stared up at me intently; he was wearing that earnest, honest frown that gets issued with the fang and the truth-serum antidote directors of films take before they talk to actors. "I give you my promise," he intoned at me gravely as he held out his smooth, soft hand for me to shake, "that no TV director will be hired for this project! My oath, my word!"

I pumped his hand, took the money and ran.

The next day when I entered the producer's office to have our first meeting concerning the script, he said lustily, "Hi, disappointing news: Floyd and Lili are out of the picture and Roger Slime has been set to direct."

As it happened, it all ended up rather well: I went back to Mike Frankovich's office, where I tore up my check into bits and pieces that I'd prudently outlined and numbered beforehand in case of a blubbering change of heart. When he heard my story, Mike voided the contract, and later the film was set up at Seven Arts. The point is that even after all of this happened, I remained Floyd's more-than-welcome guest, which would have been fine, except that really it wasn't, since the name of the guest, it turned out, was Hindley and Floyd was doing Heathcliff in *Wuthering Heights*. You think you've heard nightmares, Doctor? Wait.

The shriek-inducing perils of life with Floyd were not apparent until after pretty Lili had left. While the tasty Parisienne was ensconced, I was busy with yet another project for Sprightly and would see the bright lovers only at breakfast, or sometimes in the evening when, drawn by the sound of Floyd playing the piano, I'd amble down for a glass of wine, then discreetly withdraw or go out to find dinner. In the days that preceded Lili's arrival, I would normally slave away all through the day, and some mornings, through the mullions of my second-story window, I would glimpse Floyd stretched on a chaise in the garden tanning his upturned puckish fiz which he'd cup between aluminum-foil reflectors while butterflies crazily flapped through the air piping, "Holy shit, it's him, it's really him, I'm going to die!"

Those were the halcyon days, Your Grace. At night I would wander the town with Floyd, "roaming and patrolling the earth," one might say, and wherever we went every woman would ogle as if shot in the ass by a pygmy blowgun previously blessed by a Coptic priest. Even if the stares had been for me as well as Floyd, I would have made no moves: all my id was in my work. But Floyd's was not so easily misdirected. Now and then he'd answer back a young woman's bold stare and then whisper in my ear, "Do you think I ought to fuck her?" He'd be frowning at these times, thinking terribly hard, like Hamlet in the grip of paralysis of will, always making me uneasy, even terribly nervous, since I never knew what he was going to do next—go and offer the girl an exchange of goodies or jump up and stab some old guy behind a curtain. He often did neither. But he knew that he could have almost anyone he wanted. "Every man should be a movie star for six months," he once told me as we drove along the Sunset Strip. "I was stopped for a light by the Whiskey one night," he recalled by way of inspiration and example, "when I picked up this girl who was hitching a ride. She jumped in, did a double take and screamed, 'Floyd God!' I said, 'Right. Now how would you like to go down on me?' She thought it over for about three seconds, then reached for my fly and began to unzip me. 'Listen,' she says to me, 'I'm no fool: I'll never get another chance like this in my life.' "

The odd thing was that Floyd could be had by any woman. Once he was talking about his "instinct" that there was a "helluva film" to be made if it were built around the theme of a compulsive Don Juan—he even had the title already, *Hairdryer;* and it was then that he chose to confess he was unable to refuse any woman who wanted him. Correction—any *new* woman who wanted him. For later that night we were alone in the house when the telephone rang and Floyd answered. Some girl. Floyd mumbled through an awkward and brief conversation, then banged down the phone and cried out in disawe, which is a mixture of awe and disbelief, "I've already *fucked* her! Why would she think I'd want to fuck her *again?*" When I murmured something chideful one time about his infinite chain of one-nighters giving something of the lie to his love of Lili—Translation: "Why do *you* keep getting laid and not *me?*"—Floyd rorfled, "The difference between Lili and these women is the same as it is between cheese and shit. What the hell am I supposed to do?" he exclaimed. He stood up and put his hands behind his back, bowed his head and started pacing back and forth in extreme agitation. "I'm in my hotel suite minding my business," he huffed, "the telephone rings and I answer. 'I'm your biggest, biggest fan,' some girl tells me. 'I'm here in the hotel, in the lobby. Do you mind if I come up for a while?' I say, 'Fine.' " Floyd approached me with a glower, cheeks reddened, indignant. "She comes up and I tell her to undress. She undresses. After that I say, 'Meditate on this for a while.' She sucks me. When I'm hard I make her turn and bend over and I screw her from behind standing up. It's *impersonal!*" he roared in my face.

This shut me up for a while.

By the time Lili left, my screenplay was finished, and all of my creativeness dove to its source down in *groinus exoticus nervosus*. This was the beginning, I suppose, of the trouble, for soon I was flirting with strange young women and bringing or inviting them to the house. But I never scored. Never. Not once. Somehow Floyd would be innocuously lurking around, maybe playing the piano or just walking down a hallway, or maybe he'd cough, that's all it ever really took. My date would bolt upright, eyes glassy, thinking *Hark!* and the bullfight was over, I'd be bleeding in the sands. It always happened very spookily, like in a Hitchcock film: all I'd do was turn my head for ten seconds, and when I looked back it was *The Bimbo Vanishes*, the girl would be gone without a lipstick's trace. Well, I'd search in the powder room first, then the closets—Floyd had told me of encounters in the rest rooms of planes—and then twenty minutes later my date would appear, walking wide-eyed and dazed down the steps from Floyd's wing with this vaguely triumphant look on her face like some goofy Bette Davis at the end of *Dark Victory*. Floyd would be directly behind her at these times, perhaps to show me he was still fully clothed and zipped, although I've never been certain about this point; and once, to suggest that they had only played rummy, I suppose, he was riffling a deck of cards, a tableau that, had a prize been projected for futility, would surely have garnered my solid vote.

This began to make me nuts. Telling Floyd that this was not the way of Zen had no effect. So on nights when my date would be coming to the house, I began to conceal this intelligence from him.

"What do *you* want to do tonight, Ange?" I would yawn at mine host of the Tabard Inn as I listlessly thumbed through an old magazine.

"Oh, I dunno, Marty. What do *you* want to do?"

"Geez, I think I'll just stay in tonight and play a little auto-chess. Why don't you go out and get a hobo steak and some chili at Chasen's for yourself—right now?"

In an effort to bolster my credibility whenever I told him that I didn't have a date, I spent a number of nights at home with Floyd. These were evenings of heartbeat-skipping excitement:

Floyd would come home from his session with his analyst darkly withdrawn or just muttering "Douche," and we'd shoot a game of pool with him scowling and silent or I'd listen to his voice droning down from his bedroom as he mumbled and murmured through telephone calls from a thousand importuning women. It was like sitting at home with Hans Castorp quietly studying X-rays of lungs.

Yet my ruse went for nothing; Floyd never went out, it seemed, unless it was with me. So I started telling dates that they were not to use the doorbell, they were to wait until I came to the door. "Never mind, I'll know you're there," I would tell them; "I'm psychic." There was also an instruction to cut their engines and "coast for the final thirty yards." Sometimes I would wait for them out in the driveway, where I would make them take off their shoes and then tiptoe behind me up the stairs to my wing. It was useless: Floyd always managed to manifest, he had some kind of sonar in his dick. You want to talk about divining rods, Doctor? Spare me. At the end of his life Freud believed in the occult.

One night I was standing at the Morton's bar when I met a young actress who was sitting there alone. Within minutes it was clear that we were getting along for we had each had used *holistic* in a sentence more than once. We made a date. But I'd discovered that, as happened so much of the time, she shared her apartment with a roommate.

"Oh, so Thursday's okay?" I said. "You'll come to the house?" She said, "Sure."

"And you say you're a really good actress."

"I'm great."

One of her hands lay at rest on the bar and gently I covered it with my own in a gesture of trust and warm affection as I asked, "Could you possibly come as a hunchback?"

So. And you ask if I knew Floyd God.

When the lease on the Carrolwood house was ended, Floyd and I moved to the Chateau Marmont where I importuned the management unsuccessfully to provide me with a barricaded room. Weeks later, our film was set up at Seven Arts. They shot it in London and left me behind. From then on I wouldn't see very much of Floyd, at least not until he saved me in the matter of the cat, which, of course, was long after his deification and several years following his bodily death. Be at ease; we shall come to that part in due bazonga.

In the meantime, I first met the archfiend Zelig at the Sherry-Netherland Hotel in New York where he was wetly encamped like a snail on a peach while untangling production snafus with *Made Martians*, his film about aliens who infiltrate the Mafia. He'd summoned me to talk about some innuendoes and sexual double entendres in my script with a view to revising them for the censors. How shall I describe this vile fuck? Short, with a Napoleonic complex? He greeted me dressed in a gold silk kimono, a Cuban cigar clamped firmly in his teeth. He didn't shake hands or say "Hello" or "Want some coffee?", he just grunted and beadily looked me over, squinting with cold black fox's eyes. "I'm going to fight them," he announced to me grimly; "I'm going to shut the bastards up." He gestured to a huge composite photo spread out on the surface of a table beside him: vivid with angels and heroic nude figures, it swarmed with innumerable red circles drawn with a crayon still gripped in his hand. "Wait until I hit 'em with this," he defied me, eyes loony with triumph under squirrelly brows: "Did you know that there are eighty-seven pricks on the ceiling of the Sistine Chapel?" he boomed.

I said, "At *least*."

Is the man not an intergalactic treasure?

He is also the reason I've become what I am, Jason Hazard, the maker of arty little films that are easily financed outside of the system. Yes, Zelig was my chief inspiration, you could say. A self-made man who'd amassed a fortune leasing and selling the affordable Tirana, an automobile manufactured in Albania and sold with a thirty-second warranty on parts, he was able to establish his own mini-major, then convinced himself he knew a denouement from a bagel and was David O. Selznick's Second Coming. A Roman legion in Shaw's *Cleopatra* is described as a creature with "a single head, a thousand arms and no religion." The same can be said about makers of movies, except for the part about the head: you've got to be "collaborative," Doctor Larry, the new and entirely nauseating euphemism for artistically interferable, meaning that anyone who can speak English and has seen a few movies can be Kurosawa. But no one abused this delusion more crazily, more despotically, than Zelig. If the Leaning Tower of Pisa were a film, Arthur Zelig would tell you to straighten it up. He thought Savonarola was "soft on writers."

Directors have a Guild that can protect you from the Zeligs, but just to a point and only for a moment: you are safe until you've had your "director's cut," your edited version of the film, which you screen for a "selected" preview audience—most of it composed of the teenage group which today would call *The Wild Bunch* "precious" and an "art film"—to see whether changes might have to be made on the basis of audience reactions and comments, which of course means that twelve-year-olds re-edit your movie. And this is how Zelig always worked his will. Did you ever see a film of mine called *Voices?* It was meant to be a psycho-

ZELIG

logical thriller with a complex plot and sophisticated dialogue, and with the mayhem occurring off-screen, or even—illusion versus reality?—entirely imagined by the hero. The first clue to clear and imminent danger was Zelig's selection of the preview theater, the Seat-Rip Cinema in Torrance, a fact of aorta-icing terror second only to a numbing appraisal of the audience, which, except for some zombies from Haiti who had to be constantly admonished by the ushers throughout the running to remain in their seats, was made up of glassy-eyed adolescents, most of them members of rival gangs, and a large group of "Skinheads for the God of Job." There might have been a mummy in the audience as well, unless one is prepared to discount the report that a person looking "withered" was in line for refreshments and had asked for the "juice of sixteen tanna leaves" before grumpily accepting a Coke.

Zelig took the stage before the start of the picture, and, once he got his bullhorn functioning properly, craftily announced to the raucous audience that "the film you're about to see makes *Chainsaw Massacre* look like *Heidi*;" then, after the screening, when he'd paid for all the damages, he shot me an exasperated look and said, "*See?*"

When a film had been tailored to his satisfaction—you did it or he brought in another director—at the end of the screening of the final cut, Zelig leaped to his feet and declared to his aides, "It's going to make a profit of thirty million dollars." It went out and made a profit of twenty-three million. Zelig said, "We *lost* seven million dollars!"

I'd sold out and signed a seven-picture deal with the creep; I was insecure and felt lucky to be working at all, overjoyed to be able to direct. I even had a gross participation in the profits. How I lasted through all of those shoots, God knows, for soon Zelig was proposing ideas for scripts. Have you any idea what this meant?

You do not.

Looking back on it now, I suppose I should have had some idea of what was coming when Zelig approached me about the documentary that he proposed I should write and direct. I was to do it without any pay. "It's a short, you'll knock it off in three days," he told me; "it's a philanthropic work, a good cause, it's for Israel." Zelig was apparently genuinely furious over the press the Israelis were getting citing frequent reports of the Israeli army blowing out the brains of Palestinian demonstrators while claiming they'd been aiming at their feet. "Damned lies!" Zelig howled. "It's a goddam setup!" He explained that some Arabs in the occupied territories had been spirited to secret training bases in the desert by the PLO where their legs were being strengthened with the help of steroids while Michael Jordan and NBA players were teaching them to leap to astonishing heights with a view to intercepting with their skulls the bullets that in fact had been fired at their feet, thus inflicting embarrassment upon the Israelis. My task was to document this theory.

"Pharaonic fucks! Who the hell are they kidding?" roared Zelig, all aquiver like Lionel Barrymore in any scene in which he got bad news. "Well, they won't get away with it," he swore; "This movie will be seen around the goddam world! Fuck the New York *Times!* Fuck Michael Jordan! Let him go sell his sneakers in Trucial Oman!" Not the least stunning aspect of Zelig's mad proposal was the fact that he was neither an Israeli nor a Jew, nor had he ever given money to Israeli charities, his anger, as it later turned out, being rooted in his pathological jealousy stemming from rumors of a past romance between Sprightly and Omar Sharif's stunt double, a certain Fuad Ibn Liteupyourlife, during filming of *Irving of Arabia: The Truth,* eliciting his enigmatic warning to Sprightly, "I see you near a camel again and you're dead!" When Zelig sought to clear his ideas with the Israelis, their consulate, dumbfounded, turned him away. "Guess they didn't like the package," he grumbled at me later. "Too bad. Guess I should've gone for Kubrick. Fucking Jews."

As to what came next, may I first say that Zelig's impoverished childhood, his courage and the wit to make his mark against daunting odds, deserve a certain respect? His money hard-earned, he might spend it as he wished; but whatever inspired him to approach me with the notion of remaking the original *Franken-stein* with a monster and an Igor who were gay, not to mention their footwear, specified as "thongs," still hovers in the ether as an unsolved mystery, unless the notion had come from Jeff, a pet cobra that Zelig had raised in a tank inside his luxurious office suite and to whom, it was alleged by more than one witness, he frequently spoke, often asking for advice on nettlesome casting decisions or other creative matters, then nodding his head as if in assent to some hissing and delphic telepathic reply. Sometimes the snake showed up at screenings of the rushes.

And yet Zelig succeeded, his films made money. Can reason account for this marvel? Maybe. Once, in New Orleans during Mardi Gras season, I lounged on a French Quarter hotel balcony watching what was surely a psychic phenomenon. Below me in the absinthe streets jammed so tightly with revelers they barely could move, these thousands of people who were strangers to each other were engaged in a giddy and spontaneous conspiracy directed against a girl who had appeared from her apartment onto a balcony opposite mine. While the crowd screamed approval and urged her on, she was laughing and slowly performing a strip. When the moment to remove her bra arrived, however, she teasingly held back and the crowd took to chanting, "Show—your—tits!" again and again for several minutes while the girl shook her head but then toyed with her bra straps, giddy and coy and full-titted with power. What she did not know—and the crowd gave no hint of—was that on an adjoining balcony behind her a girl far more comely and sexy than she had already completely stripped to

the buff and was doing her impression of Fitness on Mars. In the streets a Crowd Mind had sprung up autonomously and decided to put the girl on. Zelig's secret, his knack for pleasing teenage audiences, was the half-witted brother to that: somehow, through genetics or some trick of dwarf stars, he was linked to the Universal Acned Brain.

Well, I took all I could, which I admit was quite a lot, for I'm a man of weak will and was in love with the vanities, the action, the glory of glamorous command. "What is it that drives you to write and direct?" someone asked me at a seminar back in those days. I answered, "If I don't, I feel guilty; I *must.*" Translation: "I want Table Number One at Elaine's." Ah, God, I'm a wretch, wretch, wretch, Alyosha; give me pineapple jam and slam a door on my finger. In the meantime, one other thing gripped me to Zelig:

I had fallen in love with Sprightly God.

It happened on that trip we made to Switzerland, Dmitri. We were in pre-production on *WHAT?!*, in which Sprightly plays a Rain Forest aborigine who under hypnosis by a French psychiatrist recalls repressed memories of abuse by Albert Schweitzer ("Think he'd use his real name?" the girl sneers in the script). Zelig wanted Peter Ustinov to play the psychiatrist and so had despatched us to Les Diablerets where the famed actor-author was writing a novel. We arrived in the morning to learn that the Ustinovs were invited to a party that night by Princess Grace and Prince Rainier at one of their two chalets in Gstaad. The Ustinovs checked with their hosts, who said to bring us. Shall we say that I was nervous as hell? We shall. Inside I'm still the kid from the Lower East Side. After numerous Sea 'n' Ski's on the rocks, I got disgracefully drunk, danced close with Grace and was heard at some point to utter deeply and sonorously, "Take the Princess and the Wooky to my ship!" Yes, Grushkin, your servant, the perfected asshole.

The next day, right after chocolate-fingered dawn had smeared the sky, I took a walk up the ski slope alone with Sprightly while Ustinov penned himself up with the script and his promise to give us an answer that day. It was now the off-season; few people were around. When two women walked past us, one of them did a little double take at Sprightly, but then waved away her thought with,

"No, it couldn't be her." It caused me to turn to the dumpling
and *see* her. "My God," I thought, "I'm trudging up the Alps with
a superstar, an international idol." With her openness of heart
and an unassuming reticence, Sprightly always made you forget
who she was. This was also a partial result of the Process: On the
set there is a deadly and sedated frenzy like the war room of the
Japanese carrier *Akagi* preparing to strike at Columbia Pictures,
for once you start shooting what you've got is a Ninja Turtle by
the tail with the result that your focus is singleminded, you see
nothing except what can be glimpsed through the lens. But now,
in the gullies of our silent walking, hearing nothing but the
crunching of our steps on the snow, I was feeling an unnerving
self-conscious shyness, an acute awareness of Sprightly's presence.
This is not to suggest that winning visions of *coitus interrup-
tusandyou'redead* with the woman had not previously visited my
id; I believe I might have made this rather clear once before. But
these thoughts were only fleeting bemusements, never serious,
and entirely ceased once I got to know Zelig, since the mere
contemplation of her choosing him to mate with was to prove an
invincible penile depressant. What could any woman worth having ever see in him? Fine, I've failed to mention that he looked
like John Barrymore and also had this resonant, sexy voice that
I'm sure could be seductive and terribly romantic when saying
something other than "Dick-faced exhibitors!" and "Blood-suck-
ing mongoloid IRS fucks!" But how often was that? Even
Sprightly made gifts to the colorful air. Once, while in the midst
of a soon-to-be aborted reconciliation attempt with my wife,
Sprightly asked me with an offhand but frowning concern, "And
so how is the marriage going, Jason? I mean, fuckwise." It padded
her image as the Bride of Zelig. Oh, she seemed to be a sweet
enough person, alright. Very generous. Once, when we were filming in New York, I said, "Sprightly, it's the birthday of a grammar-
school pal. He's in the charity ward on Welfare Island and I'm
going out to see him. I thought that as a present I could bring
him a movie star. You want to come?" She didn't hesitate a second.

When we got to the hush at the top of the mountain, I turned
and saw that photogenic, girl-next-door face staring thoughtfully

out at a range of Alps that were straining abortively to resemble
that breathtaking shot in *The Razor's Edge* when Tyrone Power
ascends to a summit somewhere in India and finds the Transcen-
dent, though they cut out the part where he falls to his knees and
begs God to prevent Bill Murray's remake. Her brow a little puck-
ered as if in confusion, Sprightly said the view had reminded her
of something, and she thoughtfully proceeded to recall a trip she
had made alone to the Himalayas, explaining that something had
"happened" to her there. She had met with a Buddhist monk, an
old "teacher," and together they had sat in contemplation in the
sunlight while attendants and acolytes scurried back and forth to
keep refreshing the warm, sweet drink they had given her. She
said this went on for about four hours. And then suddenly, without any signal, startling her, she saw the monk levitate into the
air. "I was sitting really close," she continued in a reverie, dreamily staring off at the snows, "and I'd guess he was two feet off the
ground." Then she turned and said quietly, stricken with guilt,
"I've never told any of this to Arthur."

I about fell down. My closest encounter with the supernatural
was hearing of a man who had a piece of net profits and thereafter
had actually received a check; anything more marvelous than that
I rated bunk. As for Sprightly, I had always perceived her thinking
to be solid and plain as a can of peas. And now suddenly this
drivel. I didn't know what in the hell to say.

Perhaps taking confidence from my silence, which, I assure you,
m'lud, was stunned, Sprightly launched upon a fervid and ranging
exploration of in-your-face whacko paranormal phenomena: astral
projection, out-of-body experiences, reincarnation, crystals, clair-
voyance, all of it the wingiest stuff I'd ever heard; but as she was
going on and on about this garbage, at some point I realized I was
getting an erection. And the loopier her statements, the harder I
got. By the time she got to "channeling" a spirit named Pareena, I
thought I'd have to jump either her or off the mountain. I had
fallen impossibly, incredibly in love!

Later I would come to know the truth about her marriage.
What had held her to Zelig was a loyal heart. He had years ago
picked her up out of a chorus line and sculpted her into a star.
Zelig notoriously philandered and during the marriage had bed-

ded more women than the Simmons Mattress Company; yet whenever Sprightly talked about divorce or separation, Zelig fell to his knees and would cry and beg, puling he would kill himself if she left him, and, at one point, in an effort to make this seem credible, he erected a gas chamber on his estate overlooking a muddy and ill-kept pond that contained a few scruffy, insurrectable flamingoes who skimmed about cursing him in guarded little grunts. At the top of the structure a neon sign repeatedly flashed the threat, THIS IS NO SHIT! But my knowledge of these matters would not come until later when at last I would steal her away from the prick.

I'm tired. Can we finish this up tomorrow? I'm getting that apple-corer headache again and I promised a man in the ward who raises moths that I would read to him from Dickens again, *Little Dorrit.* He likes it but it always makes him cry a great deal. Ah, well, "All a part of life's rich pageant." That's one of two lines that Peter Sellers once told me he would try to work into all his films; the other was "Be *silent* when you're speaking to me!"

Peter saw ghosts. When I asked him why he'd sold the home he loved so very much, he explained, "Oh, well, haunting is good clean fun, but the day I saw my socks levitating to a level that was even with my eyes I think I'd come to my limit."

Maybe he and Sprightly saw the world as it is.

Maybe there really are ghosts.

We shall see.

Tomorrow I will tell you how it all began.

Part Three

THE UNSPEAKABLE

IT BEGINS

This is out of life, out of time: an instant eternity of evil and wrong.
——T. S. ELIOT,
Murder in the Cathedral

GOD'S COMMENT TO JOB: Things could be worse.

JOB'S FURTHER POLITE INQUIRY: How?

GOD'S ANSWER: We *lost* seven million dollars!

CHAPTER ONE

LIKE THE BRIEF DOOMED burst of exploding bodies that registers dimly on teenage eyes, the beginning of the horror passed almost unnoticed; in the shriek of what followed, in fact, was forgotten and never connected to the horror at all.

The theater was the Cinema Neuf in Greenwich Village. Shabby. Underventilated. A sty. His face an El Greco of brooding intensity, Hazard paused briefly at the corner of the street, both hands in the pockets of his faded jeans as he stared with a melancholy curl of a smile at the legend on the dimly lit theater marquee: JASON HAZARD RETROSPECTIVE, it wanly announced. Under Hazard's bleak stare, and for no apparent reason, the "o" in RETROSPECTIVE came loose with a sigh and tumbled mournfully and lazily down to the street, where it landed with a damp little thud and lay still. Hazard felt the drizzle of rain on his neck, and he flipped up the collar of his brown plaid sport coat, a faded old cashmere that he'd picked up in London's at W. Bill's in sunnier times. *Okay, so there it is,* he thought, ruefully nodding: *A homage. It's official now, folks—I'm a memory.* The director bent his gaze to the shine of the street and his faintly scuffed new white Wilson tennis shoes that returned his stare and thought, "So?" Then he shrugged and moved moodily on toward the theater, slouching like Richard the Third at Easter searching out hiding places for the eggs that he'd lovingly colored and injected with cyanide, inscribing them *With Love to the Boys from Uncle Dickie.* The ominous fallen "o" was unheeded. And so often does it happen in precisely this way that the careless, unweeting soul drifts to destruction, blithe to the omens of avoidable fate.

Hazard sauntered diffidently up to the ticket-taker, who was wearing a black tuxedo. "Hello," the director murmured self-consciously. "I'm Hazard, Jason Hazard."

"Oh, of course, sir!" the ticket-taker greeted him, smiling as he put aside an inch-thick stack of "Wanted" and "Armed and Dangerous" posters that the FBI distributes bimonthly to theaters based on studies of the makeup of the youthful movie audience.

Another tuxedo, more expensive, rushed forward. Beamish, it seized Hazard's hand and shook it warmly. "Oh, so wonderful to meet you!" the florid-faced man effused. His hair gray and thinning and parted in the middle, he resembled an aging Harold Teen. "Such an honor. I'm Leslie DeWhip, I'm the manager."

Hazard looked shyly aside. "Nice to meet you."

"Had a wonderful week with your films," said DeWhip.

The director turned to him, surprised.

Avidly, the manager rushed on to describe how the theater's computer had been ordered reprogrammed to omit the comforting amenities normally demanded by the regular patrons, including the splice-breaking feature, rolling bottle effects, total loss of the center channel speaker, and the spirited recording of Mexican migrant workers loudly discussing grapes. "That's all been turned off for this week," DeWhip frowned. "We know your fans are very

different, they're not keen on that stuff; most patrons, though, without it they get scared, they think it's spooky: hearing dialogue's a shock to some people, they're not used to it." He shot a quick look at the street. "I was hoping Mrs. Hazard would be with us. Is she coming?"

"No, Sprightly couldn't make it."

"What a shame."

"She's shooting late. They're trying to wrap her film tonight."

"Oh, I see."

Hazard glanced around the lobby. "Many people been coming?"

His attempt at a nonchalant tone gasped for air.

"Nice turnouts."

Hazard's ear caught the guarded inflection, and he nodded, looking down with a glum resignation. It was then that he noticed the red felt pompoms affixed to the tops of the manager's shoes. DeWhip saw him staring. "Aren't they heaven? You just tap them with your foot and they spray out Mace," he explained. "Also sound sets them off—broken glass, certain phrases: 'Your ass!' is an automatic trigger. Incidentally, whenever we revive *The Uninvited* I always mix mimosa scent in with the Mace. So it costs us a drachma or two; why not live? *Illegible*'s just ending, by the way. How'd you ever think of making such a wonderful film about the life of Ludwig Wittgenstein's palsied calligrapher? Oh, well, it just comes, I suppose: God, talent! Well, we've got a few minutes before I introduce you. Can I get you something? Coffee? Diet Vanti Papaya?"

"No, I'm fine. I think I'll stand in the back for a while."

"Watch out who you talk to."

Hazard moved mournfully into the theater where he stood and watched silently from the rear while the ending of his film flickered past him like a life. As with all of his later, deeply serious work, it had been shot in black and white, but in a wide-screen format, and featured the usual trademarks of his style: the extensive use of hand-held camera shots panning dizzily from close-up to close-up, and the long and intensely searching looks between the actors that generated dialogue pauses so extended that entire novenas could be said between lines. With the lone exception of critic John Simon, who described it as "banal as graves in a row"—a barb blunted by the knowledge that Simon, an eyewitness, had used those very words to describe the Resurrection—the national reviewing establishment adored it, in particular a critic for Time magazine who discerned in it "a meditation on gaps." The shooting of the film had been marred by tragedy. While on location in the Roman catacombs, Hazard had designed a spectacular mirror shot utilizing thirty-eight mirrors in all, and in the process had somehow managed to lose in the infinite maze of reflected images an Italian lighting double, an ever-smiling youth known only as Gino, who up to this date had yet to emerge.

Hazard watched as the last of the subtitles faded, mentally re-editing the film even now. A perfectionist, obsessive and compulsive in his craft, he'd spent a year and a half on *Illegible*'s assembly, spawning many versions and a fistful of endings before his exasperated, maddened distributors ripped it from his grasp with cries of *"Basta!"* and "Hold the anchovies!" all around. And now as the Rachmaninoff end title swelled—Hazard always used classical recordings for his scores, for they were cheaper, not to mention their fragrance of chi-chi—he felt once again that same self-hugging joy as when he'd first seen the film in its final form. At the fade, the applause was tumultuous, wild, and for three entire seconds Hazard felt happy. Then a curious confusion and despondency sapped him; the fallow years had somehow changed him, and his body of work, it often struck him now, was fraudulent, trivial and shallow. *Why were there subtitles here?* he brooded. *What was I thinking? The actors speak English.*

Now the manager breathlessly loped onto stage, whereon a spotlight, befuddled at first and faintly cursing, caught up with him and exhaled a sigh of relief. "Ladies and gentlemen . . ." DeWhip began smartly.

With his head bent, Hazard slowly moosed down the aisle. The manager's lavish introduction droned on and when Hazard at last had achieved the stage, the applauding audience sprang to its feet as *Bravos* popped up hotly like flowers in the sun.

Soon Hazard was sitting in the famous old chair in which Spanky McFarland had once been incontinent, and, after a diffident greeting, he disconsolately brushed at a confetti of questions: some of them from fans, some from students of film and still others from masked and mysterious assailants who asked about scenes that were not in the films and then stubbornly continued to assert their existence in spite of the director's repeated denials, a phenomenon peculiar to art house homages, if not to the bowels of Caligula's warships whenever the discussion of the rowers turned to film and it happened that the emperor himself had come aboard, which always seemed to stir an ambiance of giddiness belowdecks.

Toward the end a young woman near the front raised her hand. "You've been favorably compared to a number of the greats," she drawled—"Kurosawa, Goddard, Debris—yet you haven't made a film in several years. Why is that?"

Hazard answered her immediately and bluntly. "I can't get financed. My films don't make money."

He pointed to another raised hand near the back. A young man in pajamas stood up. "Can you think of any reason why?"

"Why what?"

"Why your films, as you say, don't make money."

"Well, maybe they're just terrible films," shrugged Hazard.

Loud demurrals from the crowd, from the curtains, from the seats. Then, morosely, the director gave another explanation. "Harry Cohn said, 'Give the people what they want and they'll turn out.' Well, my films don't seem to do that. It's as simple as that."

"Do you think you'll ever change your approach?"

Hazard tightened his jaw. "Never."

Whom the gods would destroy, they first make stupid.

"So you're wrapped?"

"Yes, it's done," Sprightly wearily answered. "How'd the tribute go, pie? Was it fun?"

Hazard nodded. "Yeah, I guess," he said glumly. "It was fine."

They were sitting in a booth at the crowded Stage Deli. Hazard lifted his irritable gaze to the crush. "It's the stateroom scene in *A Night at the Opera*," he groused. "Where the hell is a goddamn waiter?"

Sprightly's miffed stare drilled the space above his shoulder.

"On a crummy little shot of me opening a window, that shithead did twenty-seven takes with a thirty-five lens, another twenty or so with a fifty and a whole bunch more with a seventy-five. Can anybody tell me the fucking difference? This business is disgusting. It's yak shit. I hate it." Her gaze fell to Hazard. He was scowling, looking off in his search for service. Sprightly pushed her mammoth-sized sunglasses back with the tip of a finger and cleared her throat. "I've been thinking of quitting the business," she announced. "I think I'd like to have a baby. What do you think?"

"There he is!" the director declared, oblivious. He flung up his arm to a passing waiter.

"Yes, yes, in a minute!" cried the waiter. He sounded and looked like Jackie Mason. "I'll be back, I swear to God, my solemn oath, I'll be back!" He knifed toward a cluster of Guardian Angels in front of a display case, defending the lox, and disappeared into the sea of their camouflage clothing.

Hazard scruted the Angels with hooded eyes; the low drone of their murmured ritual chanting of "Make my day" was getting on his nerves. He turned and gloomed down at the table again.

"Did you hear what I said before, Jason?"

"No, what?"

She looked at his finger tracing patterns on the tablecloth, the despondent slump of his shoulders. "I said we should have gone to the Carnegie instead."

"I checked it. The line was almost three times longer."

"Then Elaine's. We haven't been there in years."

"No, not Elaine's." He shook his head. "Not there."

Sprightly put her hand over his and squeezed. "Poor pie."

His gaze shot up like a blow. "Look, I couldn't care less," he gritted intensely, "that I can't get a goddamn picture off the ground, or that today you're all the rage while I'm totally dicked, or that you work all the time when I can't get arrested. *That is never on my mind,*" Hazard ended up shouting, *"and has nothing to do with not going to Elaine's!"*

"Oh, God," Sprightly breathed in a pained aside. Among the tables and the booths blank faces turned.

Someone coughed. Hazard shifted his menacing stare to the tall and mango-complected presence who was sitting in the booth with them next to his wife and wore gold lamé robes, a purple turban and dangling rhinestone scimitar earrings.

"Ralph, get the fuck out of here," Hazard warned quietly.

"Sahib not happy with live-in guru?"

The accent was singsong New Delhi.

"No, sahib not happy; sahib tired of you, Ralph, very tired of home movies of your family in Nepal always gasping for air with their eyes bulging out and then clutching their throats while they smile for the camera."

"Sorry, sahib."

"Stop calling me sahib."

"Better bwana?"

"Hindu fuckface."

"Jason, *leave him alone!*"

"Do you have to take him everywhere, Sprightly?"

"I don't!" she gritted.

"Can't I eat a pastrami on rye without having to consult the *fahkockte I Ching?*"

Sprightly's cheeks blossomed flame, her lips thinned. "He was with me on the set, I just brought him," she said tightly.

"Why the hell does he always have to be on the set?"

"Ralph guards my dialogue, shithead!"

"From what?"

"From acknowledging the power of evil forces!"

"Jesus." Hazard looked away and shook his head. He saw their waiter whooshing by and grabbed his arm. "Could you bring us some menus, please, pal?"

The waiter peeled away Hazard's grip. "You want menus, three blocks over you can find a computer store, bubi. Here in Grace-land we are short on high tech." His droopy gaze flicked inscruta-bly to Ralph, then back to Hazard, where it lingered for a moment in unreadable appraisal. "I'll be back," he uttered tonelessly. He then flew into a martial-arts crouch and hissed *"Hatai!"*, but just as suddenly fell sullen again as, shaking his head and checking his order pad, he pythoned off amid a haze of grumbles.

Sprightly eyed the bin of kosher pickles on the table, lolling dills that were exultant and gleamy in their juice. "You should have said you're not casting today," she said dryly.

"I thought everybody knew that."

Sprightly's head snapped up. She looked stricken.

"It's all over for me, kid," the director smiled crookedly. "Face it—I am now Mr. Sprightly God."

"You are *not!*"

"I haven't even had an offer in years."

"Because they know you're so particular!"

"I'd direct my own funeral if they asked me."

Eyes bulged. Ralph and Sprightly turned their heads to one another, locking gazes that hummed with an ominous foreboding like the Morse code message at the start of *Gunga Din* ("The lines are down . . . I don't like this"). Sprightly's mind plucked a thuggee pick from the wall.

She turned to Hazard with her hands clasped together on the table. "Pie, you're going to get an offer very soon," she said gravely.

"What offer?"

"Never mind. Just don't take it."

"Don't take it?"

"There'll be better."

"Look, I won't direct your pictures."

"I know that."

"So what offer?"

"I don't know. But it's coming and it's dangerous . . . evil."

"Evil?"

"Ralph saw it in a vision."

"I have seen it," lilted Ralph.

"Don't accept it," Sprightly warned. "It's Satanic."

"Truly, sahib!"

"Dammit, Jason, quit laughing!"

"*How?*"

The waiter was back and in hover, full of bustle. "As requested, *Dead Souls* and *The Brothers Karamazov*," he announced, thrusting menus at Sprightly and Hazard, then mourning, with a dismal look at Ralph, "Lord Shiva, our miserable and craven apologies: our menu in Sanskrit is in use at the moment, Sonny Bono dropped in with the Dalai Lama."

Behind her glasses Sprightly's eyes made darting searches of the room.

"And now your orders!" brisked the waiter, pen and order pad poised.

"We're going to need a few minutes, I think," Hazard murmured.

"We are open all night, Prince Mishkin; dawdle."

When the waiter's bleak gaze shifted over to Sprightly, she had taken her sunglasses off to read the menu. He froze, staring numbly with his mouth agape like a starstruck blowfish in the grip of hypnosis. "You're Sprightly God!" he rorfled.

Sprightly looked away, breathing, "Shit!"

The waiter's glance went to Hazard.

"Are you anyone?" he pinned him.

"No, I'm no one."

"Her agent?"

Sprightly grabbed up the bin of pickles and tossed its contents in the waiter's face. "He's a world-famous movie director, you asshole!"

The waiter looked at Hazard. "Any parts for a Jew?"

The Hazards and Ralph found the street, walked some blocks, then ate grilled cheese sandwiches with mustard at the Prexy's next door to the Plaza Hotel. Afterwards they commandeered a horse-drawn carriage out front because Sprightly felt sorry for the horse.

"Pie, they really need the money," she said.

"But, sweetheart, the money doesn't go to the horse, it goes to the driver," Hazard explained to her in a quiet, reassurring voice, as if fearful of rousing a dangerous maniac.

"It trickles down to the oats."

The horse, who overheard this exchange, thought to speak but then decided that he liked his life immensely and did not care to trade it for a television series.

On the clopping, slow ride to the Hazards' apartment, a fine mist of rain again moistened the night, and except for the instance in which he asked Ralph for the meaning of the Malcolm X button on his turban (Ralph's answer was "Those who know do not speak, and those who speak know only sambals"), the trio clutched stubbornly at sulky silence, tugging it up to their necks like a shawl. But as they exited Central Park to Fifth Avenue, Ralph sniffed the air like a worried hound.

"Poo-poo vibration now feeling, evil doo-doo."

Hazard glanced toward the sound of a taxi being hailed; with a screeching of brakes, it swerved to a canopy just to the right of their passing carriage.

Hazard gaped. "Holy shit!" he emitted. He looked stunned.

The hailer of the cab, a tall man in a trenchcoat, paused to follow Hazard with his stare for a moment, and then silently entered the cab. It sped away.

"What is it? What's wrong?" Sprightly worried. "What happened?"

Hazard's gaze remained fixed on the dwindling taxi. "That guy who grabbed the cab. I could swear . . ."

"Swear what?"

"Well, I could swear it was Jesús Machtmeintag."

"That's impossible, Hayzoos is dead."

"Are we sure?"

"Sure, we're sure. You're imagining things."

"Sprightly, how many people do you see on Fifth Avenue wearing a Prussian army helmet?"

She paled. "Oh, my God!" she breathed.

Hazard nodded.

Jesús Pedro Machtmeintag was a mysterious cinema projectionist with whom Hazard had briefly feuded at the time of the exclusive Manhattan running of *Autumn Nocturne*, his film about Brahms, or, more precisely, Brahms's thoughts while deciding which pen he should use while composing the Brandenburg Concertos. On the evening of the critics' preview screening Hazard had attempted to enter the projection booth to check the sound and the brightness of the image, since too often the expenditure of grueling hours perfecting the balance of the sound track recording and the density and color gradations of the film were rendered void by the whims of a theater projectionist, or, more often, his masters' greed, as when he drastically lowered the brightness of projection in order to lengthen the life of the bulb. Most especially with opening exclusive engagements, Hazard's practice was to worry the theater projection booth each night for perhaps a week, making sure, in the interest of maintaining picture focus, that no literature in Braille was kept around, and that the volume of the sound track would not be turned down on the sole complaint of a flea circus worker, a tuner of microscopic harps whose strings were made of hair from wrists, and was seated in the very first row and had a migraine. Hazard, after all, was a man who had once spent several days in a soundtrack-mixing room to ensure that his audience would hear, amidst the beckoning of competing auditory distractions—a breeze, the distant klaxon of a train, the main dialogue—the dull, whipping *fff* of a single poppy as its petals uncoiled and snapped into bloom. But when Hazard sought to enter the projection booth during *Autumn Nocturne*'s opening engagement, he discovered that the door was inexplicably locked. Hazard rapped on the door, but no one answered and at first he heard nothing but silence from within; but when he leaned in and pressed an ear to the door, he heard the faint whispery, whirring sound of sprockets engaging surreptitiously. It maddened him. He pounded on the door. With shocking suddenness, a viewhole came uncovered from within and a bloodshot, baleful blue eye glared out.

"What zer hell do you vant!" the eye's owner demanded in a deep low bass that rumbled threateningly while Valkyries stood by and held its coat.

"I'm Jason Hazard, I directed the film."

"Too bad."

"Too bad?"

"Never mind; you tried."

Hazard's breath came short, his neck reddened.

"Open up," he ordered tightly.

"Vat zer hell do you vant?"

"I want to check things. Let me in."

"No, you *can*not."

"I *can*not?"

"I need *lebensraum*. Ziss iss *my* domain."

"You're saying no?"

"No, I am not saying no—I'm saying *nein!*"

Down slid the viewhole cover with a snick.

Livid, the director stalked away and fetched the manager, a bored, airy redhead named Bingo Nonpareil.

"Who is this schmuck?" Hazard asked him.

"Jesus. He only works here on Sundays. Very touchy."

"Jesus?"

"Yes, he's Bolivian; an Amazon Indian, I think."

"He sounds German."

"Oh, well, doesn't he? Doesn't he?"

Just as they arrived at the door to the booth, the sounds heard from within—the metal cranking of a reel being manually wound, someone tenderly humming the "Ode to Joy"—abruptly ceased as if swallowed by an absolute vacuum. Hazard and the manager exchanged brief looks, and then the manager essayed the door. It was locked.

"Jesus? Jesus, it's Bingo," he called. "Open up!"

From within came the rich, refined voice of a black man. "No Jesus in here," it demurred. "Just us brothers."

"Booth okay," declared a Japanese female. "Go away!"

"I have a bomb!" warned a Middle East accent.

"Oh, bullshit," drawled the manager. "Come on, now, Jesus, open up!" He rolled an exasperated eye to the director. "He does voices," he commented archly. "Clever."

Ethel Merman belted "Everything's Coming Up Roses," the strident voice piercing the metal of the door.

Exasperated, Nonpareil rattled the doorknob. "Come on now, cut it out, Jesus! You're singing crap!"

"Go avay!" shrieked the deep German voice hysterically. "You haff zer wrong man, I tell you! I am innocent!" There followed vociferous and adamant denials that he'd ever gone bowling with Joseph Goebbels, weekend flying with Rudolph Hess, knew anything whatever of the letters of transit or had ever defaced *Casablanca* posters to suggest the film's hero was Conrad Veidt.

"All lies!" bellowed Machtmeintag in a fury.

Suddenly the door to the booth burst open, revealing a powerfully muscled man, a giant with an eyepatch, one blazing blue eye, a bronzed skin, gypsy earrings and flamboyant bandanna that concealed the major portion of a radical crewcut. He was wearing a color-splashed shirt from Hawaii and behind him, on a hook above a splicing table, hung a spiked Bismarckian German army helmet that dated from World War I. Ripping open the shirt in a spray of loosed buttons and tearing a hula dancer in half, he bared his chest and shouted, "Shoot me! Go ahead! You haff judged me already, so shoot! Ziss iss *Oxbow Incident,* only more stinky!"

When the manager threatened the projectionist with job loss, the director was sullenly admitted to the booth where, ignoring the black and red paper bunting festooned above the photograph of Heinrich Himmler (an inscription read, "To 'Jesús' from 'Jose'—hah hah hah!"), Hazard ordered the glowering Machtmeintag to maintain illumination at sixteen lamberts and "for chrissakes, be sure you don't miss any changeovers," statements that aroused a look of death unseen since Medusa unwrapped the gift of a snood from Perseus at Christmas. But as Hazard snooped and checked around the booth, the projectionist did not utter a word but rather shifted his menacing gaze to the floor, content to hum softly in an ominous undertone the strains of "Lili Marlene," an unsettling performance repeated each Sunday during the entire run of the film. After that the anonymous death threats began, messages fashioned from words clipped from newspapers, one of which was finally traced to *La Prensa,* the single word "Gringo," which, it happened, appeared in the inaugural note, coupled closely with the English admonishment, "Die!" There were telephone calls with only breathing on the line, or sometimes what seemed to be recordings of tanks that rolled on and on until Hazard hung up. Additionally, innumerable pack-

ages arrived, most containing shredded fragments of a film by Hazard with a note reading, "Excellent changeover, ja?" One parcel contained the final reel from *Autumn Nocturne*, but completely re-edited and with a new soundtrack consisting of the barking of a tether of dogs being fed and cajoled by Zsa Zsa Gabor. In the package was a copy of Eliot's *The Waste Land* and a note reading, *"Datta. Dayadhvam. Damyata."*

These attacks would continue unabated for years, but on a date that coincided with the fall of France in World War II they abruptly ceased. A few months into this peaceful season, Hazard saw Nonpareil at a preview. "How's Jesús Machtmeintag?" he asked him. "Oh, he's dead," said the redheaded manager languidly, exhaling cigarette smoke to the side. "An accident at sea, I understand. Something freaky."

According to the manager's laconic report, the projectionist was last seen boarding a cruise ship chartered by a shadowy organiza-

tion that called itself Bolivians Indentured To Christ. The ship
and all its passengers and crew disappeared while traversing the
infamous Shapiro Triangle, leaving behind no sign of its passage,
with the possible exception of a black leather bag found washed
ashore in the Cayman Islands that contained only strudel, some
tiny whips and a handwritten note on the personal stationery of
the wife of Field Marshal Goering inviting the receiver, "Mein
Zeus!", to play bridge. In addition some clippings—bad reviews of
Hazard's films—were discovered together with a note in a bottle
on the beach near the Fontainebleau Hotel in Miami, reading,
"your turn next, stinky jew director!"

"Do you think he meant you?" Nonpareil had asked Hazard.

"I'm not Jewish."

"You're not German, though; isn't that the point?"

The clopping of hooves upon pavement was hypnotic. As he
gloomed into the mists with arms folded on his chest, Hazard felt
a vague sense of foreboding. He shivered.

"Machtmeintag's definitely dead," reasoned Sprightly. She

turned toward the moody dark clumps of the park. "Funny how he went the same way as Floyd," she mused. "Maybe they're somewhere together."

"You think Jesus had a girlfriend?"

"I imagine," said Sprightly. "Why?"

Hazard glowered. "I hope she's there with them."

At five the next morning, the director sat hunched in his penthouse study sipping coffee from a thick white porcelain mug while he labored on the script that he'd been writing for years, something easily accessible to quantum physicists. Now and then he'd glance at his telephone sourly, thinking of his agent, Tony DeSky, who had long ago taken to neglecting Hazard and regularly spoke to him through an assistant whose only other duty was to cancel lunch dates. Loath to dismiss DeSky through the mails—their relationship spanned almost thirteen years—Hazard was attempting to fire him by phone, but the agent had yet to return his calls.

The director's gaze sullened up to a window and the Empire State Building's glowing tower as he hopelessly wished for King Kong to appear with a captive DeSky clutched screaming in his hand while the other hand was cupped to his gash-red mouth as in thunderous voice he boomed out across the canyons of the city, "Hey, Hazard, I *got* the fuck!"

"*Meow.*"

Hazard scowled as he glanced around at Barbra, Sprightly's bushy and beloved Himalayan cat who was good only for puking, attacks of the vapors and attaching designer hairs to his shirts. Frozen in the doorway and inscrutably gauging Hazard through whiskers that gave her a look of perpetual crossness, she struck one as the fruit of a summer's dalliance between a disgruntled Cheshire cat and a yeti.

Hazard stared hatefully.

"Scat! Get lost, or I'm turning you into a tiny rug!"

Abruptly Barbra bristled, and her hair stood on end in a stunning imitation of a Halloween cat. She hissed and spat in the direction of the telephone.

It rang, a jangling shock in the stillness.

Hazard snatched the phone from its cradle.

"Hello?"

He heard a muffled roaring sound in the background.

"I hope I didn't wake you," growled someone with a boozy voice that had the texture of sautéed sandpaper. "Sorry. I had kind of a wakeup call myself. From Arthur Zelig. I'm calling from the plane. I'm flying in."

"Who's this?"

"What do you mean, who's this?"

"I said who is it?"

"Are you shitting me? It's been that long?"

Hazard gasped. It was Tony DeSky!

"I've got a red-hot offer for you, Jason. You'll love it."

The lights of the Empire State Building flickered, frantically signaling a message in Morse:

Do not listen, Jason! Do not listen!

But who takes advice from tall buildings?

CHAPTER TWO

"AND HE WANTS ME to direct it?"

"That's right."

"Something's wrong," Hazard brooded.

"Nothing's wrong."

"The book's the hottest movie property in years; why would Zelig want to do me any favors?"

"He likes you."

"He wants me *dead!*"

"Not that much."

"I stole his *wife,* for chrissakes! Are you drunk?"

"I don't know yet, it's too soon to tell."

Hazard's agent popped free the top button of his shirt, tugged down on his necktie and checked his watch. "Yeah, way too soon," he blearily murmured, "it's not even nine o'clock yet, what's the panic?"

He'd come in on the red eye and had taxied immediately to meet Jason at the Plaza Hotel where they sat by a window now in the Oak Room while the agent transmitted the dumbfounding offer from Hazard's archenemy, Arthur Zelig, to direct a film to be based upon *The Satanist,* the notorious occult novel by Jonathan Drood that had petrified the planet.

Hazard frowned. "Why the hell would he do this?" he puzzled. He slipped off his navy blue Burberry raincoat and placed it on the back of an empty chair.

DeSky bit off the end of a cigar and lit it. An unflappable, loosely draped soul in his forties, he resembled a benevolent Groucho Marx looking out upon the world through horn-rimmed glasses as if at a pleasant but curious dream. Serenely, he sipped at his third martini and then set down the glass upon the whiteness of the tablecloth with what less than reckless judgment might deem to be somewhat excessive care; it was a movement that was sluggish yet discontinuous, like interrupted slow-motion.

He turned and put his arm across the back of his chair and then responded in his gravelly rasp, "He's eccentric."

"He's commitable, you mean."

"Oh, well, colorful."

"A man talks to snakes and hears them answering in Latin and he's nothing more than *colorful*, Tony?"

"And so what do I tell him?" the agent asked blearily. "What do I say to your new best friend?" He hiccoughed demurely into a hand.

Hazard shook his head and stared down at his coffee.

"Something's wrong," he said darkly again.

"Nothing's wrong. You want a job, you keep saying. Here's a job. Every goddamn director in the world wants this gig."

Hazard lifted his head. "Look, I don't direct trash."

"No, you don't direct anything these days."

"Oh, and whose fault is that?"

"You mean it's *mine?*" DeSky raised a bushy, black eyebrow in amazement, if not with a thought of crying out, *"Police!"*

"Why the hell do I have to even *think* about this garbage?" fumed Hazard in an injured, resentful tone. "I've got a wonderful movie in mind, a sure winner; all I need is the chance to make a pitch, to set it up. Where the hell are the meetings, Tony? Where've you been?"

The agent lowered his head and peered over his glasses. "Listen, how many meetings have I sent you to, Jason?"

Hazard picked up a menu. "Never mind, let's forget it."

"Did I set up lots of meetings for you, Jason, or not? I mean, I wanna get this straight. Did I send you in to people who could greenlight any project?"

"That was almost two years ago, Tony."

"That's right, Jason—word gets around."

"About what?"

"About how you piss people off."

"Would you kindly explain that for me, fuckface?"

DeSky crooked his arm atop the back of chair. "Okay. You want to hear?" he offered expansively. "Here it is, here's your whole M.O.: You go in and make a pitch for your original, right? They deflect it politely; they kiss your ass, in fact, and after that they explain *their* idea. You hate it and you tell them all off, you put them down; that's why you're there, that's why you come to these meetings in the first place, just to crap on these people and show your contempt. Now am I right?"

"No, I never did any such thing."

"Not directly. But what do you call it when they ask you to think about a possible mini-series based on *The Fly?* When they ask you real nice and polite and deferential and they say you can make it really dark, really deep."

"Look, I went to that meeting just out of politeness."

The agent's eyelids drooped to half-mast. "You went and suggested that The Fly by day should be a restaurant inspector for the New York Board of Health."

Hazard turned and stared stonily out through the window.

"Those people admired you, Jason."

"Let's forget it."

"They liked you."

"Okay, so just once I lost my temper."

"And what was it that you lost right after Columbia passed on one of your favorite projects and you pitched them to finance a movie called *Sieve* about a condom-dispensing machine that's possessed?"

"I said *forget* it."

"Then because Dawn Slutsky's at the meeting and she sends us all these pro-abortion fund-raising letters, you decide you're going to make it a double feature and you pitch them the sequel, *Delayed Reaction*, where a woman kills her forty-seven-year-old son so the ACLU can prove in court that a woman's offspring is a part of her body."

"That idea was mostly serious," Hazard piously objected.

"Your alternate title was *He Was A Pain in the Ass Anyway.*"

Hazard bowed his head into a hand.

"Is this makin' any sense to you, Jason? Tell me. And then there was your plot about a second gunman, you told them, the night that Bobby Kennedy was killed."

"*Lots* of people think there might have been a second assassin."

"But do any of them say it was Joe DiMaggio?"

Hazard's head snapped up. His eyes blazed.

"*Those fucks! They had it coming!*" he erupted in a fury.

Shocked patrons nearby turned their heads, all but a frail and very elderly woman who beckoned to her waiter and then quietly asked into his ear, "Which fuck are they discussing? Is it Zelig?"

The agent's empty glass was slipped away by a waiter and a fresh martini set down in its place. "Hey, thanks a whole lot," slurred DeSky at the waiter. He raised his cigar in an affable salute.

"Will there be anything else for either one of you gentlemen?"

"Jason?"

The director bowed his head again and shook it. The waiter padded off to less perilous fields.

DeSky lit his burned-out cigar with smacking puffs and gazed benignly at a woman in a bright yellow rainslicker passing by the window. "And so, great," he rasped musingly, summing up; "and so now you're persona non farta worldwide and throughout the known universe. Right? Yeah, that's right. But then now comes salvation, a chance to start over, and right at the top with a huge bestseller; a chance for a monster commercial hit that would make you employable again, you understand? You want to think about that for a coupla minutes? Go ahead. I'll just sit here and goof around awhile."

Hazard looked up and stared off towards the park, his features softened by puzzlement and doubt. "Why the hell would he do this, Tony? I don't get it."

"He thinks you'll bring a skeptic's approach to the material, Jason; you'd make it seem a lot more realistic."

Hazard turned away from the window and glowered.

"That's your fourth different answer to this question, Tony. You're becoming a one-man Rashomon."

"Listen, didn't we do *this* a million years ago, Jason?" The agent had crossed his inner wrists together, miming a ritual exchange of blood. "Have I ever steered you wrong? Take the gig, for chrissakes."

"He wants Sprightly for the mother?"

"That's right."

"She's afraid if I direct it something terrible will happen."

"Something will: you'll stop collecting unemployment."

"Tony, please don't get smart."

"*Someone* has to. How does Sprightly come to know about this gig, by the way?"

"Her guru told her."

"Her guru?"

"Her live-in *cook* and guru."

"Oh, where did she find him; through an agency, Jason? Got the number?" DeSky groped around in his pockets. "I think Patsy could use one of those at the beachhouse."

Hazard lowered his head into a hand and breathed, "Jesus!"

The agent abandoned his search for a pen. "Yeah, okay," he said, "I'll have to get the number from you later. In the meantime, would you take this fucking gig, for chrissakes? It'll put us back in business again."

"I can't do it."

"Why can't you?"

Hazard's head came up. "I won't direct crap."

"It's not crap."

"Yes, it is."

"Have you read it?"

"I don't have to," snapped Hazard. "Are you kidding me, Tony? A kid who gets possessed by some devils?"

DeSky held up a tempering finger. "Only one."

"It's preposterous!"

"Listen, do this fucking picture," whined the agent. "Just do it! It's a guaranteed, stone-cold smash and the worst that can happen is you'll make a small fortune, and the best is that you'll find yourself employable again. Take the job! Why the hell are we kockin' around?"

Hazard turned and looked out at the rain-bloated sky with his stomach and his face and his brain afire: he ached to have the stones of temptation turned to bread, to hurl himself from heights into angels' hands and then accept a smoking pen and ask, "Where do I sign?"

Want work! Will work for food! drummed the rain.

"I don't know," he said uncertainly.

"Come on."

"I don't know."

"So what's the downside?" growled the agent. "What's to lose? Take a meeting with the guy and see what happens. I think he's got something in mind you're gonna like."

"There's no script," Hazard faltered. "I'd have to see a script."

"You'll see a script."

Hazard turned to him, his eyes crammed with doubt, and for a moment he observed in incredulous silence as the agent tried to balance an olive on his nose. It fell down on the table, rolled a little, then was still. DeSky picked it up without comment and munched it.

"What's his concept of the picture?" Hazard asked. "What's his take?"

"Who gives a shit? You're directing it, you'll make it what you want."

"I've got to know what he's thinking."

"Take a meeting."

"Sprightly's going to be a problem."

"Take two."

After pouring his agent into a taxi, Hazard made a visit to Doubleday Books around the corner from the Plaza on Fifth Avenue where he wedged on a pair of dark glasses before going in to purchase a copy of *The Satanist*. He conducted the transaction in silence, conveying the impression he was either mute or in telepathic contact with the rulers of Mars; and to suggest that he was buying the novel as a gift, he scooped up a number of clothbound copies of works by Pascal, Kierkegaard and Camus, plus the title *He Said He'd Be Back in Half an Hour*, an obscure reminiscence by a Merrilee Crater. The clerk at the checkout made no comment.

At the penthouse, Hazard entered the apartment stealthily. Sprightly and Ralph, he could tell, were in the kitchen discussing the merits of various chutneys; he could taste their voices as he padded to his study, where he locked the door, reached into his plastic Doubleday bag, plucked the novel from its quaking and relieved companions ("Holy frig, that was scary!" emitted the Camus, which had stood untouched for months on the shelf between *Nancy Drew and the Mysterious Statue* and Norman Mailer's *The Naked and the Dead*), sat down at his battered and yellowed pine desk with a notepad and sharpened pencils handy, then started to read in the desperate hope of discovering some core of implicit integrity that he could bring to the fore and transmute. But by the end he'd found only a throbbing headache. *This is scary?* He couldn't get past the basic premise. It was ludicrous. He simply couldn't do it.

Could he?

"He's got something in mind that I think you're gonna like." Really? What was it? And why? Hazard wondered.

No good, came the instant and ominous response. Zelig never forgave or forgot an injury, or even an imagined slight. A vendettist for all seasons, he would mutter in his pillow each night until he felt he had exacted his revenge, which was often delayed and unusually complicated, and pursued at no matter what cost, not even of further hurt to himself, as had happened when Hazard once refused to shoot a scene that Zelig had written. Zelig waited for the film to be completed, then simply refused to have it screened for the critics, thus creating the inevitable prejudgment that the film was too awful to survive a review, an impression which Zelig himself helped to further with anonymous tipster calls to the media, in which he would identify himself vaguely as "someone involved with the Zelig people" who wished only to "do the right thing for art." For columnists he added "exclusive" quotations such as, "Hazard said the media are scum, Sinatra's right."

This cost Zelig many millions, but allowed him to climax in his sleep seven times on the opening weekend. "Fuck the grosses," he smiled as he dreamed; "this is living!"

What could he possibly be up to? Hazard puzzled: *Is he born again? What? What the hell is in his mind? Is he counting on me not do the picture? Is that it? Is that Step Number One in some weirdo plot of his?*

He determined he would have to find out.

Hazard got up and slouched to the kitchen where Ralph chanted mantras while simmering a curry. Sprightly's mood was one of clouded and suspicious apprehension. "So what happened at the meeting, pie?" she asked him; "What's the deal?"

About to make a surly and defensive response, the director saw his guilt and shame fall on luck in the form of a stack of identical books that were sitting on a desk beside a clutter of mail. Pouncing on this chance to project his sins, Hazard seized the top copy with chagrin and irritation, growling, "What the hell's this, a damned channeling book?"

"We've got lots of them."

"But this one you *wrote!*"

Still smelling of cardboard box, it was a crisp advance copy, just arrived from the publisher, of *I Used to Not Believe in All This Shit.*"

"Cut the crap," Sprightly rorfled. "You look guilty. What's up? What did Tony have to say? What's the offer?"

The director's defenses collapsed and he told her. When he mentioned the novel, Ralph's eyes whited open and he stared as if into some Vedic hell, perhaps the locker room of Rudyard Kipling's club.

"The goddamn *Satanist?*" Sprightly erupted. "I don't even want that book in the freaking house! It's jinxed! It'll bring us only trouble!"

"Ah, come on!"

"Tell him, Ralph!"

"Book is evil, sahib—badness!"

"That's a crock."

"Floyd's friends, the Montenegros, bought that book," squalled Sprightly, "and their house burned down that night!"

"And you think there's some causal connection?"

"What's it *look* like?"

Hazard shaded his face and murmured, "Jesus!"

"*Don't curse!*"

He gave her a look and walked away. As he exited, he flung to those behind him, like a horrifying curse or a live grenade from hell: "*The book is in the house!*"

Sprightly shrieked.

Ralph moodily turned to study her with his saffron-coated gaze. "Do not worry," he bangled her with absolute assurance; "there will be no such meeting with this Zelig. I have seen it."

Hazard took the next flight out to L.A.

Part Four

AH,
MEPHISTOPHILIS!

CHAPTER ONE

MUFFY PELTZ, ARTHUR ZELIG'S assistant, was a honey-haired, san-
daled, full-lipped tan wearing glasses, no makeup and a Bryn
Mawr drawl that devoured half the content of anything she said.
When she ushered Jason Hazard into Zelig's office in one of those
Century City towers that resembled the boxes that Disneyland
had come in, he saw in an instant that little had changed: the
mogul, in the clutch of a telephone call, raised a hand in unsmil-
ing, flaccid greeting, inadvertently brushing it against the tassel of
the red and black Shriner's fez he was wearing along with the
green silk Ninja robe starkly rampant with AMERICA—LOVE IT OR
LEAVE IT! admonishments in red against a blue and white background. The impenetrably dark sunglasses were new, however,
Hazard noted with a quiet headshake, as was also the tightly
layered wrapping of bandages entirely encasing the mogul's head.

"Brufishwumfawfummshthaza?"

The director turned blankly to the waiting Peltz. Guessing
wildly that either he'd been offered coffee or a deconstructed
passage from *The Turn of the Screw*, he said dully, "No, thanks,"
whereon she nodded and buttocked from the room to his relief.
Still awhisper in his phone conversation, Zelig motioned the director to a pink suede loveseat facing his oval-shaped teakwood
desk, a huge island near the center of a massive room whose
ceiling was studded with rotary fans, their wooden blades turning
drowsily with nightmarish slowness as they pined for warm gin
and the company of tsetse flies and the voice of the British raj.
Warily, Hazard sauntered over and sat. A vague cloud of foreboding had settled upon him. Outside, California sunshine blazed,

thinking, "God, I'm so good to the avocados," but the office was immersed in a Gorkyan murk: all of the drapes and shades had been drawn and the ghostly glows from a few scattered lamps provided the room's only pallid light, those and the neon wash from the snake tank mounted on the side of Zelig's desk. Jeff appeared to be asleep; no coil stirred.

Hazard's gaze ranged slowly and incredulously upward to a giant photograph of Sprightly affixed to the wall behind the desk, a shot from *Miracle* with Sprightly in a spacesuit and a caption at the bottom reading NEVER AGAIN!; then his stare slipped inscrutably down again to Zelig. The mogul's rich, resonant voice had changed: he now spoke in a husky, eerie whisper that, along with the bandages and dark glasses, evoked Claude Rains in *The Invisible Man*. *What the hell is he up to?* winced Hazard, confounded. He noticed several Dustbusters plugged into walls. More newness. Then his glance caught a cane atop the desk.

"Yes, Ed," the breathy, ominous undertone continued. "The rushes were beautiful. Really. Simply great: the sets, the lighting, the camera—everything. Wonderful! Marvelous! Simply first rate! I'm so grateful, Ed. You never let me down, you're true blue. Above all it's your loyalty I treasure, my friend." Zelig's head now turned subtly in Hazard's direction. "Yes, loyalty. 'Who steals my wife—I mean, my *purse*—steals trash,' et cetera et cetera blah-blah-blah. 'And now I must bid you—an affectionate—farewell.' " This last, intoned with a Virginia accent, replicated Robert E. Lee's last words of an address to his vanquished Confederate troops.

He's gone, Hazard judged him, *completely bananas; he's lost the last card he ever had in his deck.*

Was this the simple answer to the mystery of the offer?

Zelig hung up the phone and turned around to face Hazard, though his stare seemed to aim a full foot above his head. "So— long time," he raspily husked. "Awful lot of water under the bridge, Miss Ilsa."

The attempted Dooley Wilson imitation and homage to *Casablanca* fell on silence.

Abruptly the mogul stood up with a clatter. He fumbled for the cane on the desk and picked it up. "Can I bring you a refreshment, Jason? Name your poison." For a moment Zelig froze and Hazard thought he heard, "Shit! Bite your tongue!" beneath his breath.

The mogul turned his head to the side and uttered, "Jules?" From somewhere a grunt and then a growl emanated, then the sound of some animal shaking itself. Zelig's hand reached down and out of sight behind the desk, and when he'd walked around front he was clinging to the guide-harness grip of a seeing-eye dog, a German shepherd, who looked dazed, if not sedated. On the end of his snout was a thought-provoking Band-Aid. For a moment Zelig stood there, motionless, a phantom, as if waiting for his audience to drink in his fact; then he rasped in that spectral, husky whisper: "Do you see what you've done to me, Jason? I'm blind—blinder than a blintz in a barrel of batshit. It happened on that day you ran off with my Sprightly. They tell me that it's psychosomatic. Hysteria. Who cares? Do you really care,

Jason? It's done. I'm having a Kir. It's after four. Will you join me?" He leaned forward and down toward the dog a little way, coaxing softly, "The bar, Jules. Good lad. To the bar."

The dog lurched forward and immediately barged into an antique end table next to the sofa, upending a lamp, and from there it veered left into Hazard's couch, recovered, banged its head against Zelig's desk, then blithely steered him into a coffee table, where a Chinese vase fell and shattered. Hazard propped his elbows on top of his knees and wordlessly lowered his head into his hands. He heard further sudden crashes and bodily thuds intermingled with soft *oofs* of pain from Zelig and muted little whimpers and grunts from the dog. After this came a period of heavy silence. Then Zelig said quietly: "Where are you?"

Hazard looked up. The mogul stood mute and immobile in front of an alcove bar.

"I'm right here, Arthur."

"Are you sure you won't join me?"

"No, thanks. Maybe later, though."

"Of course."

Hazard watched him as he expertly mixed a Kir, and then took

up the guide-harness grip again and collided into walls and objects of furniture prior to reaching his enormous desk and sitting down without spilling a drop of his wine. The dog curled up and closed its eyes.

"I don't know what I'd do without Jules," Zelig mused. He sipped at his drink and set it down on the desk with a dull, wet click of glass on wood. "Do the bandages disturb you?" he rasped.

"Operation on the eyes?"

"Not at all. I've had plastic surgery. I want to look like LaToya Jackson."

Hazard stared.

"Are you sure you won't join me in a drink?"

"No, I'm fine," said Hazard numbly.

"Very well, then. Let's cut to the chase." He leaned forward. "The material is foolproof, Jason; indestructible, a smash, a guaranteed, balls-out hit. And that's what you need now, lad. Bottom line. You need—" he paused, and then finished portentously, but in a guarded, low tone—*"The Satanist."*

The dog raised its head with a growl, hackles bristling. Zelig turned his head toward the sound and was still, then turned back and resumed his discourse with Hazard. "You're wondering why," he whispered hoarsely. "Why would I give this plum to you, this treasure that will make you hot again?"

"That's entered my mind," answered Hazard.

"I need you, Jason. It's as simple as that. I still despise you, you traitorous fuck, and deeply hope your judge in heaven will be Vlad the Impaler. But nothing must stand in the way of this need of mine. It's only business now, Jason; just business. But may I ask a question, old shoe?"

"Go ahead."

"Before you ran off with her into the night, were you already in escrow with My Lady of the Channels?

"What happened to business, Arthur?"

"Dickology preempts business."

"Well, it's none of your greasy concern now, okay?"

"We're getting testy."

"What in shit do you want from me, Arthur? How is it that *I'm* the one you need?"

"The truth?"

"If this material's so great, why in hell would you need me—or any other director, for that matter? Why don't you direct this piece of brilliance yourself?"

Zelig gasped, and then uttered, "Thy prophetic soul!"

Now the mogul craned his head up, lifting his chin and thus resembling Major Hoople in a hospital burn ward posing as a sightless Delphic oracle, possibly the Sibyl of Cumae, on a drunk. "I *have* always wanted to direct," he rasped, his Shriner hat's tassel atremble. "Now I can't, of course; and yet I can. Yes! With your help I can do it! I *will!* You're the greatest technician in the world, the nonpareil, and I will settle for nothing less for this venture, for this dream that I have nurtured ever since tothood on first beholding *Captain Blood* from high on a peak in fucking Darien!" He was alluding to the second balcony of a theater in southern Connecticut. "Jason, can you guess what I'm coming to?" he frothed. "Do you see it? Do you grasp the point?"

"No, Arthur. I don't."

"*You* will be my eyes!"

"I'll be what?"

"You will be the ostensible director. But behind the scenes it will be *I* who calls the shots; yes, on everything: the wardrobe and the casting and the script; on the hiring of the crew and the whole enchilada!" He had risen very slowly from his seat in a rapture, his stiffly curled hands outstretched and upraised like Eduardo Ciannelli in *Gunga Din* as he vows that his hordes will engulf all of India. "I will choose every head of department," he raved, stunned spittle spraying out at the air; "every extra, every grip, right down to the writer!"

Hazard was hypnotized, struck dumb.

Abruptly, with a move of blurring swiftness, Zelig sat and was instantly placid and urbane. "Yes, of course, you'll get the credit and the money and the fame," he husked with the calm of the Sargasso Sea, "but in my heart I'll know *The Sat-*"—Zelig caught himself and turned toward the dog, which had snapped its head up warily, ready to react—"in my heart I'll know the film is really mine," he ended saying.

"Well, I can tell you—"

"No, no, stop, now! Don't say it, Jason! Listen! No one else will ever know of this arrangement. I swear it! You'll have legal protections: liquidated damages of ten million dollars should the press ever mention one word of this deal."

"Oh, Arthur—!"

"I said hear me out, Jason! Just wait! Let's assume that I'm wrong, for a moment. Alright? Assume that—for the sake of discussion—I'm insane."

"Assume?"

"May I speak without these constant distractions? Little nitty-shitty barbs from the uttermost depths that contribute no visible light to our times?"

Hazard turned away his head and sighed, "Yeah, go ahead."

"This is all in your interest, Jason."

"Right."

"As a backup, I will give you a three-picture deal with a budget of up to twelve million per film."

The director turned to Zelig, nonplussed.

He said, "*What?*"

"You'll make anything you want with complete control, no approvals whatsoever—carte blanche: any cast, any crew, any subject, any script, any quirky self-indulgence you may choose to inflict upon us. Am I being sufficiently frank?"

Hazard gaped.

"Yes, Jason?"

The director felt giddy, ill. When he started to speak, he felt his voice begin to crack. He stopped and then started again with a quaver, "How in hell could an arrangement like this be kept secret?"

Zelig clasped his hands on the desk and hunched forward. "On the set there will no communication," he confided. "After rushes, when the others have all gone, we'll confer. In the meantime, of course, I will be the producer. No one would think my input strange."

"They wouldn't?"

"Are we starting with this pissiness again?"

"Why does Sprightly have to figure into this?"

"She's the best for the part and you know it. That pixieness plays against the horror of events. Incidentally, without her we have no deal."

"You wily prick."

"Do I take it that's a yes?"

"You take nothing! Do you really think I'd let you dick around with my film?"

"*Your* film? You said you hate it, Jason. How could it be *yours?* As for dicking around, why, it's just like the good old days: I mean, actually—what would be new?"

Hazard flushed. "Who's the writer on the project—you? Are you going to be the fucking auteur on this, Arthur?"

"Are you mad?"

"Well, I wouldn't put it past you."

"That's absurd. This is meant to be my masterpiece, Jason. Who knows how long I'll live to try again? These operations." He delicately touched at his bandages, murmuring, "I wonder if LaToya will sue."

"I need approval of the writer," Hazard said suddenly, hearing the words as if someone else had said them.

"Well, then, mutual approval. Alright? We can settle this now, in fact," cooed Zelig. "Are you willing to pre-approve Jonathan Drood?"

"Drood? Drood himself is going to do it? He's agreed?"

Jonathan Drood was the prince of horror and the best-selling author in all the world. Hazard's objections to his work were philosophical. Drood's talent was beyond any question: everything he wrote, without exception, was a hit.

Zelig nodded. "He's agreed. It's a seven-figure deal. You can see that I'm going first cabin, can't you, Jason?"

Hazard frowned and looked down and shook his head.

"There's something wrong with this," he murmured.

"Nothing's wrong."

The instant after Hazard had departed from his office, Zelig swivelled to the snake tank and rapped on the glass. "Jeff? Are you awake? Did you hear? It's proceeding: Step One of the Plan is underway. In addition, we're on schedule and under budget: we got him a town car instead of a limo. In the meantime, by Monday the trades will be announcing that Faust has been signed to direct—" There was a pause, and then he finished: *"The Satanist."*

The terrified dog snapped its head up from slumber and with a snarling wet yelp sank its fangs into his leg. The mogul absorbed the event, sitting motionless, then spoke quietly. "I'll remember that, Jules."

CHAPTER TWO

TAPED MEMO TO FILE

Wednesday, August 7, 1994
Subject: Jason Hazard

HAZARD'S WIFE WAS IN to see me again today, this time, however, at my request. I had hopes that she could lucidly fill in the gap between Hazard's fateful meeting with her former husband and the ultimate decision to go to California for the purpose of filming the novel, *The Satanist*. It's a—what's going on out there? Some kind of a disturbance outside, wild dogs, or maybe cats, in a frenzy. Okay, now it's quiet again. As I was saying, Mrs. Hazard came in at my request since her husband's account of the period in question comes down to his insistence that a "being of light" had suddenly appeared to him on the roof of the Chateau Marmont where he was pacing and mulling Zelig's offer, and gravely advised him to "take the gig." Wearing white robes and an Alpine cap, this being materialized a piano, Hazard claims, briefly played it, then suddenly vanished, but leaving behind him as proof of his visit a golden calling card that stated, "This is to confirm that you have had a personal and vivid encounter with the Angel Ravelli."

My repeated requests to see the card have been deflected.

Transcription of Session with Mrs. Hazard

Doc, I know you're going to think this sounds crazy and stuff and I guess that would be fine except it actually isn't on account of I'm certain I am absolutely right that the universe is traveling to someplace, it's a person. The greatest, biggest thrill the world can give is from shtupping, which of course is meant to keep the human race from dying out. Well, that's purpose. But purpose is the business of a mind. Get the picture? Who invented the *idea* of the orgasm?

Doc, I'll get to Jason in a minute, okay? but just now try to think about *this* for high concept: In order for a universe like this to exist, the kind that can nurture human life, means that back in the beginning of things, Big Bangwise, the force of that very first outward explosion had to match the opposing force of gravity with an unbelievable accuracy of just one measly part in about one billion to the sixtieth power, which is the accuracy you would need if you fired a bullet at a one-inch target at the opposite side of the observable universe, which is twenty billion light-years away. And there's the primordial bacteria thing. The primordial bacteria were jaunty-jolly with an oxygen content of the atmosphere at no more than ten percent. But for jillions of years they kept busting their asses to make double that amount of oxygen, which was very bad for them but good for us, which is weird, because we hadn't even come on the scene yet and how could the bacteria know that we were coming unless the whole universe has a mind? So when you stop to really think about stuff like that, what's the problem with me saying I was once a great pharaoh in a previous life and was shitty to my slaves?

Later on I'm pretty sure I was Torquemada, but I'm paying for that now, I think; well, just a little. Anyway, I thought we ought to get things straight before I heard any channeling jokes and I decked you. Okay? I'm just not in the peachiest mood.

What a world—first Floyd and now all this. Poor Jason. I knew this was coming—Ralph saw it. Ralph tends to come through on this stuff, I mean seerwise. He ought to: he communicates with dead people constantly and *some* of them should know what's going on, don't you think? Anyway, you wanted to know about some things, like what happened when Jason came back from L.A. and—Start with that? Well, he had this different look about him, Doc; he seemed wired. It was subtle, you know, underplayed— just a little extra bulging in the eyes, a little shine, like when *Action*'s called and buildings start exploding in the background and you freeze and completely go up on your lines. "It's alright, I can make the thing work," he froths. "I'll just make it as a meta- phor, sweetheart, a twenty-first-century allegory of the existential- ist dilemma, the good- versus dark-world forces embattled. Noth- ing *really* supernatural is happening at all," he raves on; "the whole thing is entirely subjective! All the paranormal happenings are symbols of changes, evolutions, going on in the souls of the cast! It's the same as with *Lear* and the storm on the heath, which was meant to be a mirror of events in Lear's mind, the fucking macrocosm matching and reflecting the microcosm! They're just Jungian archetypal forms!"

"Any tits and ass?" I interrupted him.

"We don't *need* them!" he shouts. "We've got *demons!*"

Oh, well, shit. I mean, I pleaded and I pleaded and I argued. Then I told him, "Go ahead, do what you want, I'm sick of yell- ing, but I won't play the mother, Jason, no way. You go and do this on your own and we'll just pray you stay safe." So he tells me that there isn't any deal unless I star. "Oh, well, doesn't *that* make you have to wonder?" I told him. "You and Zelig? That's all his- tory," he says to me, "a memory." Then he pulls a contract from his briefcase—*signed!* I fell into a chair. "Jesus, Mary and Joseph," I told him, "You've gone and made a deal with the devil!" "It's okay," he says; "I had the lawyer check it."

Dumbfounded, sitting with Barbra on her lap, Sprightly gaped at her husband with mounting dismay.

"First I'll have to research it, of course," he thought aloud.

Sprightly squalled, "You said research, Jason? Research?"

"Black Mass, Missy! Voodoo!" Ralph warned from a doorway, his lips still moist with tandoori chicken. "Research bring evil spirit in to us, sahib!"

"Ah, that's dork! If The Satanist—" Hazard began. But no sooner had the dangerous words been uttered than the cat's fur

fluffed and bristled into wire, a phenomenon soon to be totally eclipsed in the breathless daring of its conception as Barbra, in a generous bravura performance, hissed and spat flecked foam prodigiously, emitted a bloodcurdling cry, then gazelled from Sprightly's lap to the wooden floor with the grace of Sabu the Elephant Boy high-diving from a cliff into a blue lagoon with a Honda Civic strapped to his leg. She landed on her head and side with an "Oof!", got up dazed and then clattered from the room on clumsy claws.

"It beginning!" doomed Ralph with wide eyes. "Spirits coming!"

Oh, well, I didn't know whether to piss or go blind. Then I flashed on a night about a few months back when I woke up in bed and saw that Jason wasn't there. I found him sitting in the library running old films—his own. He didn't see me, he was totally lost and absorbed, and he had this kind of funny sad smile on his face, like he was looking at something from his childhood that he loved that was never coming back, never ever ever ever. I went back to our room, got in bed and cried. Now I looked in his eyes and I could see he was dying. So what could I do, for pete's sake, be a cunt?

"Do I have to see Zelig?" she asked him.
  "Not once!"
  "Closed set?"
  "Armed guards."
  "I want priests!"
  "You want priests to keep Zelig off the set?"
  "I want priests to bless the set!"

I remember when that would have turned Jason on. He's built up an immunity to whacko, I guess. I just wanted to grab him and yell in his face, "Hey, I want to quit acting! I want to grow up!"

Most of all what I wanted was to have a baby.

This business. All these interviews with starlets on the tube always mentioning how much they love a challenge in their parts, as if a life filled with cancer and earthquakes and war and drive-by shootings isn't challenge enough; yeah, we need some heavy-duty stuff like, "What's my motivation?" You hear all these speeches at the Academy Awards, you'd think we'd found a cure for cancer or done something great. Oh, well, kiss my ass, you guys, and then maybe you'd have what you really want. Doing something kind, that's what ought to get Academy Awards; generosity of spirit and stuff, self-sacrifice, not hanging up on wrong-number dialers; also not standing in somebody else's key light the way Edward G. Robinson did to me. Time after time in the middle of a shot I'd be thinking, "How come all of a sudden I'm so cold?" until finally I realized he was standing in my light. Those wily old icons, they knew all the tricks.

I'd like to do something terrific. But I'm dumb. At least that's what creepy Arthur used to tell me all the time; he used to yell at me, "You're dumber than that fucking Egyptian!" Okay, so I'm really not that smart, I admit it, and I never went to college or any of that stuff so I don't know how to do something useful and important, like patching up a leg that's been broken, or a heart, or discovering milkshakes all over again. Oh, yeah, sure, I can act and maybe hoof a bit and sing, but I never heard of Jesus saying, "Blessed are the starlets." I think He said "Visit the sick," not "the set." Yeah, my books but so what, for pete's sake, what's it mean? So I figure there's just one important job I can handle that really means diddly-dick-all in this world, and that's to have kids and to bring them up right. When I was twelve and I went to this camp in Vermont, the last night every kid would trudge over to the lake and put a little floating candle down onto the water and we'd watch them all drifting out into the darkness and lighting it up a little bit for a while. Well, that's what I want to do now with my life. Jeesum, Jason could be such a big help if he'd get straight, there's so much he could teach his own kids, he's so smart. He could teach in a college, too. I wish he would. Do you think I've kind of rationalized this thing? Could be this urge to have a baby would be there no matter what, whether bringing up kids was a good thing or a bad thing. Isn't that right? It's biological and stuff? Ah, shit, there I go again, crying, goddammit. Jesus, Doc, I want a baby so bad, I really do, but I'm scared it's all slipping away. I'm thirty-seven. But then Jason and that look in his eyes.

So pathetic. So I didn't say a word about the baby. Blessed are they who have projects in turnaround.

I bought a humongous gold cross to take with us so Jason could wear it on the set in Fornicalia. Ralph said that actually it had to be silver, but I put in a call to Christopher Lee and he told me, "Look, darling, whatever works." So we went for the gold. Out in Malibu we rented a house in the Colony. It was right on the ocean and all, but kind of spooky, a tight Cape Cod with these huge dark beams up high and these old plank floors that creaked; Jason said he needed to be put in the mood.

The Colony turned out to be a pain in the ass. Twenty million dogs run up and down the freaking beach all day and they pretty much crap their brains out, all of which dumps right into the water, which not only is filthy but freezing cold so you never even think of going in for a swim. And then there were the assholes running horses on the beach, and the bimbos in bikinis auditioning for Jason. Yeah, for Jason. You could look up and down the whole beach all day long and you'd never see a girl doing somersaults and handstands, only when they walked past the house, swear to God. How'd they know that a famous director lived there? But the worst thing was Malibu was basically boring. The only bit of juice was living next to Larry Hagman. You know? J. R. from *Dallas?* Him. Every sunset there'd he'd be out in front of his house in kabuki robes and a Viking helmet and whenever the sun had gone down really pretty, Larry always used to stand there for a while and applaud it. I liked that a lot.

Tony, Jason's agent, lived a few doors down and he was also really fun and kinda cute, in a way, always clumping in barefoot

and burned from the beachside and dropping cigar ash all over the tar while he had a few beers and got plastered and shmoozed. I had a feeling that he liked to get away from his house, on account of twice a week it's completely invaded and the other five days of the week it's a mess. Tony's wife is a sweetheart, really a doll, but she stays in this upper room painting all day and she hasn't got a regular maid, she's got this crew of eleven confused-looking Mexicans who used to be mechanics in Nuevo Laredo, all of them related to one other—"It's a package deal" is how Tony described them once, his eyes all bleary and hooded—and they come twice a week in this open truck and then swarm around the house like Keystone Cops, always yelling *porqué* and creating confusion and getting almost absolutely nothing clean. Patsy keeps them on because she says she feels sorry for them. "Who else would hire them, Tony?" she tells him in this helpless little voice, her eyes saucers. "How would they live without us? They're so helpless." So Tony clams up and just drinks a lot of Heineken in other people's houses.

Anyway, now we were there and unpacked. I was scared. I mean, really, I was worried to death. Arthur was up to something, something fiendish. This whole thing was weirdo, it gave me the creeps. Jason said, "Relax, there's no conspiracy, he's looney-tunes." Sure, but that didn't make him any less dangerous. Crazy, not crazy or out of the body, Arthur doesn't forgive and he doesn't forget. He's after my Jason, I just feel it in my gut.

Poor pie: he had nothing to do with the breakup. I'd decided to split long before I'd even met him. I never loved Arthur. Oh, well, for ten minutes, maybe, and under false pretenses. I had this little part in a Broadway show when Arthur came backstage—that's how I met him—and he said he'd like to test me for the lead in a film. I was blown away: a big mogul! the movies! The next morning I'm back in the theater for the test and my heart's going ninety-seven miles an hour while me and my new best friend, Arthur Zelig, are standing there alone onstage with scripts and a boom mike floating over our heads: Arthur'd brought in a crew and was filming the audition. I was reading the lead and him all the other parts, and I was nervous as hell, I was shaking like a leaf, when Arthur reaches out his hand and gives mine a little touch on the top, a gentle brush, like a tender reassurance. Well, I guess I had a meltdown right there on the spot: I was in love, or Svengali-struck, or whatever; let's face it, I was only eighteen years old. When I brought it up to Arthur a year or two later, it turned out he'd blown spit on my hand while he was reading and just wanted to wipe it away before I saw it. Yeah. And then Arthur's chicks, of course; he had more of them than Rossum had Universal Robots, maybe even more than Floyd, God rest his soul. I know he screwed more waitresses than Floyd because I'd keep finding mayo and A–1 on his shorts. How he did it gives you some kind of glimpse into his soul. Arthur thought he was impotent, you see. Oh, well, the whole thing was actually psychosomatic: Arthur's what you'd have to call a hysteric, I mean, shrinkwise. Another thing is Arthur's a hypochondriac. In the hospital once for exhaustion from constantly lying to Army Archerd, he says to me, "Death must be close to my bedside, I'm getting a burn from the radiation. I burn real easy." Yeah, he did. He'd get a burn from standing close to a hot director, or Brazilians, or if someone said "beach house" too loud. Anyway, he had this idea he was impotent, so he got himself some medicine for it and just before sex he'd say, "Hold it! Time!" and he'd give himself a shot of prostaglandin in his dollylocker with this hypodermic needle from Thrifty's and then as he got hard he'd say, "Whoopee!" and stuff, or just stare and shake his head and mutter, "Science! Science!" Sometimes he'd sing "That's Amore." The thing I never got is how he handled his one-nighters. Arthur's thing was being suave and in complete command, very cool, all romantically Charles Boyer. Can you see him in his office doing casting couch numbers? "Oh, Miss Peltz, bring in a one-cc syringe and a swab, would you, darling? Oh, and hold all my calls for a while." I've tried to picture him making out in back seats of cars. "Could you please hold this flashlight for me a second? Okay, shine it right here— no, no, *here*, Gaia, *here*." Almost anybody else would have given up screwing. Not Arthur: Arthur went and got this painful operation where they put some kind of implant inside of his dick so he could bring it up to speed for as long as he wanted and without any stage waits any number of times. Arthur will do anything to get what he wants—anything, no matter what it costs him, he's relentless. Which is why I was so worried. Yeah, the book, the book was evil, it was definitely trouble. But mainly it was Arthur. What was he up to? Oh, sure, now we know. But then?

It was scary.

Part Five

GREENLIGHTED INTO HELL

See, here are Faustus' limbs
All torn asunder by the hand of death.
The devils whom Faustus served have torn him thus.
For twixt the hours of twelve and one, methought
I heard him shriek and call aloud for help.
  —CHRISTOPHER MARLOWE,
    The Tragical History of Dr. Faustus, 5.3

Let the good times roll.
  —ARTHUR ZELIG

CHAPTER ONE

SIX WEEKS INTO PRE-PRODUCTION, Hazard was manically attached to a desk in his office at Prep 'n' Save Productions, a provocative office rental complex on Hollywood's bustling Fairfax Avenue. No space was available at Zelig's studio lot where three features were currently shooting; they were scheduled to move there in two or three weeks. In the meantime, the dankness of the company's encampment—its soiled gray walls and rickety furnishings—added a dullness to the temper of the air. Hazard's mood was one of restiveness and annoyance. For one thing, he had just had a bitter encounter with the number-one sandwich maker at Canter's Delicatessen, who'd refused to put mustard *and* Russian dressing on a hot pastrami-chopped liver combo on rye. "Vat de hell, are you crazy?" he'd huffed. "Dot vould ruin it! Normal people wouldn't even *tink* of such a ting! What am I having here already, *Conversation vit de Vempire?*" The waiter brought the sandwich to Hazard undressed, with separate sides of mustard and Russian and a note reading, "Try to find another place to eat."

The other hound nipping at Hazard's soul was the worrisome lack, thus far, of a script. Open on his desk was a copy of the novel. The director had been marking off sections and scenes that he believed to be essential for inclusion in the film, and certain work, such as set design and special effects, had already been launched and was well underway. But Jonathan Drood had not been in touch with him, nor had Hazard been able to find him. "Listen here, Jason," Zelig had soothed him, "the school of genius has always been solitude. The lad [Drood was only twenty-eight] wants to make the thing perfect, his best. So be grateful.

And be calm. We are destiny's tots. The script will be ready whenever it is ready. In the meantime, the movie is the novel—work from that."

Hazard looked up from the book and out a window, brooding at the CBS Television Building as it pinkly drowsed in the morning sun. His creative instincts were feverishly churning just as if the project were entirely his own; now embarked, he was determined that the film should have grace, and he would give it his usual obsessive attention down to the finest detail of craft. All the heads of department, chosen by Zelig, had been hired and some were already at work: a British production designer, Dennis Reek, was creating the look of the Georgetown house wherein most of the film would most likely be shot; and a special-effects man from Europe, Franz Detritus, was devising levitation and other effects in reliance, like Reek, upon events in the novel, which was deeply preoccupied with things in midair.

"So."

Hazard turned to the whiskey voice, ruddy face and perpetual scowl of Tommy Gruff, the white-haired, crusty production manager planted by the desk with fists on hips in his customary vaguely truculent manner as he scrutinized Hazard with testy eyes that glowered under bushy Falstaffian brows. Stubby and muscular, he had recently given up alcohol and a heavy smoking habit and thus was constantly on edge. Yet he gave Hazard comfort: the first to be selected and hired by Zelig, Gruff had worked with the finest of the world's directors and on countless classic films.

Hazard turned around in his chair.

"What's up?"

"Look, about the location stuff in Georgetown. I had a conversation with Mrs. Mahoney this morning and . . ."

"Who?" Hazard interrupted him.

"Mrs. *Mahoney*," Gruff erupted on him irritably. "Jesus, try to take a stab at *listening* now and then! She's the owner of that house by the steps," he ended sullenly.

"Oh."

"Yeah, *oh*. Well, she says it's okay for us to shoot and all that, but we'll have to build a dummy east wall out in front so the window looks closer to the steps. That okay?"

"Better check it with Dennis."

"What the hell do you think I just *did?*"

"Well, I think it's okay, then."

"You *think* or you *know?*"

"I know."

"Let's *hope,*" Gruff rumbled darkly. He turned and walked out with a shake of his head, his shoes scraping carpet with a sound like grumbles. Hazard's secretary entered with a thick white porcelain mug of hot coffee that she set on his desk.

"Oh, good," Hazard told her. "Any Equal?"

"I put it in already."

"Thanks, Millie."

Frowning, she leaned over the desk and spoke softly. "Someone's waiting to see you," she imparted uneasily. "It's a Jesuit priest. His name is Vogel."

Hazard glanced out the open door to Millie's office. On the sofa sat a redheaded priest in his forties. With a long and sensitive face and sharp features, he was quietly absorbed in *The Hollywood Reporter.*

"He says that Mr. Zelig told him to see you," Millie continued in her hushed, troubled tone. "He's going to be the technical advisor on the film."

Hazard quickened. *The Satanist's* references were Catholic, but before he left New York the director was frustrated when, in the course of his intensive research, he found himself unable to locate any Catholic priests who had actually performed an exorcism, or even witnessed one. Maybe Zelig had finally found one for him.

"Show him in, Millie," Hazard said eagerly.

"Yes, I will, sir." Millie seemed doubtful.

From his desk Hazard watched as the secretary minced to the outer office and approached the priest. "You may go in now, Father Vogel," she told him.

The Jesuit looked up, set down the paper and said softly in a quavery voice, "That's right." His tone had been vaguely defensive and combative, and he held her stare for a moment challengingly before peering in mutely at Hazard. Then he rose and walked slowly into the office, his wary gaze taking in the room before he stopped near the desk and appraised the director with cold green eyes that bored like lasers and ceaselessly shifted from side to side in minute and rapid, nervous darts, as if constantly searching for offense to be taken, if not a grievous and mortal wound. He exuded an aura of paranoid danger.

"Father Vogel, I'm Jason Hazard. Glad to know you."

The director had stood up and come around his desk with his hand outstretched to shake the priest's hand. Vogel looked down at the hand without comment, then appraised the director's face for a moment, nodding slightly and then tremulously breathing out, "Right," in a tone that suggested some troubling reservation, some haunting shadow of a doubt. He reminded the director of the actor Scott Wilson doing his *In Cold Blood* killer act.

The priest reached out and took Hazard's hand, held it absolutely motionless for a time as he stared at it silently and inscrutably and then dropped it without any comment.

Hazard paused, uncertain what to make of this, and then gestured toward a sofa facing his desk. "Please sit down, Father Vogel," he offered uncertainly. He turned, went back to his desk, sat down, then looked up to see the priest hadn't moved. He was immobile, fixedly staring at the sofa.

"Is this where you want me to sit?" he asked tonelessly.

"Sit wherever you feel comfortable, Father."

Vogel turned and appraised the director unreadably, then looked back at the mango-colored sofa and finally nodded his head, breathing, "Right." After sitting, he looked down to the side at the cushion, pushed into it twice with stiffened fingertips as if checking out its firmness and then turned his lowered head to the front and mutely shook it.

"Is the sofa uncomfortable, Father?"

"I'm here now."

"How about that chair by the window?"

"I'm here."

The priest then lifted a stare at Hazard that seemed to suggest he had abetted the Fall. The director was beginning to feel uneasy. "Well, now, listen, it's good to have you with us," he essayed. "I'm going to be needing lots of help."

"That's right."

The director took a beat. "I'll want the saying of the Mass to be impeccably correct: the proper vestments of the day, the right moves, the whole thing. Then of course there's the exorcism itself. Have you ever done or seen one, Father Vogel?"

The priest's kaleidoscopic green gaze searched the air for a time with their darting, rapid flits. Then he said, "Yes."

"Oh, that's wonderful. I mean—that's really good; that's a help. Have you read the novel, Father?"

"Why should I?"

The director was momentarily speechless.

Vogel leaned menacingly forward toward the desk with his eyes jigging madly as they searched Hazard's face. "Any reason why I should?" he rumbled dangerously.

Hazard stared at him mutely, flustered. "Gee, I guess that *was* a pretty dumb question," he fumbled. "Hey, of course you wouldn't need to read the book; why, you're extremely well versed in these matters."

"I'm extremely well *what?*"

"Well versed—you're an expert on possession."

For some moments Vogel seemed to think it over, his head at an angle and tilted upward while his eyes darted rapidly back and forth in a scan of the infinite possibilities. Then he nodded and looked back down and told the director tersely, "Right."

Something cataclysmic had just been avoided.

Hazard uneasily shifted in his chair.

"Where'd you study for the priesthood, Father?"

Once again Vogel's eyes probed the wounded air while his right hand fumbled in a jacket pocket. "Maybe Woodstock," he quaveringly offered. "Or St. Andrews-on-Hudson. Does it matter?" From his pocket he extracted a can of Dos Equis beer and popped the lid with a flick of his thumb. "Does the laity really even *give* a good damn?"

"No, maybe not," the director said hastily.

"Right."

Vogel tilted back his head, gulped beer and then wiped away froth from his mouth with a sleeve.

"I didn't think so."

The priest set the can on a coffee table while his other hand groped in a pocket and then fished out a package of Marlboro filters.

"Every seminary's just like every other," he said testily. He tapped out the last cigarette in the pack.

"I would think so," said Hazard in a toneless voice.

"Same thing all over. They're all alike."

Vogel popped the cigarette into his mouth and then lit it with a flame-throwing yellow Bic that bore the logo of the Universal Studio Tour. Now Hazard saw the 82nd Airborne tattoo—there was a tiny blue parachute above the inscription—vivid on the back of the Jesuit's hand. The empty packet's cellophane crackled thinly as the priest crushed it up and stuffed it into a pocket.

"I've been told that possession in America is rare," the director said numbly, utterly transfixed.

"That's a crock," Vogel sneered. "Total crud. There are exorcisms going on all of the time."

"In America?"

"Where are we sitting now, jughead? Right now, this very second, you can bet there's an exorcism happening somewhere in the U.S. of A.!"

The director leaned back in a wary flinch. "I've been told," he said cautiously, "there've been maybe only three formal exorcisms by the Church since the nineteen twenties."

Vogel grabbed the beer can and put it to his lips. "Huh-uh," he grunted, his eyes still on Hazard.

"You're kidding me."

Vogel shook his head, still gulping, then lowered the empty can of Dos Equis and effortlessly crumpled it up in his hand. "I am?" He leaned forward with a baleful stare. "Well, let me tell you something, wiseass," he began with a smolder: "I do exorcisms every freaking day of the week. I do them constantly, my theater is never dark. Blacks, whites, Hispanics—I don't give a rat's ass, if I find out there's a demon in the creeps, I throw him out. At the start I sort of slap 'em around once or twice." He exhibited a fist: "Death without the sacraments. But if they're tough I try the old rubber hose and then hit 'em with the prayers in the Roman Ritual and flush 'em from the victim like a dose of salts. And that's the whole thing, that's the drill, that's how I do it."

He tossed the crumpled can into a wastepaper basket. "Two," he breathed softly. He stood up. "Guess I'll see you 'round the set," he told Hazard menacingly, his eyes alive in a deadpan face. Then he exited the office, pausing in the doorway to ask, "You want this open, chief?"

Hazard quickly shook his head.

"Whatever Lola wants," said the priest. He then pulled the door shut in silent slow motion, his burning green gaze fixed on Hazard to the end.

Hazard slumped. Then through the door he heard the Jesuit's voice: "Do you keep any beer around this place? Cigarettes?"

"No, Father, we don't," Hazard heard Millie answer.

"Well, then, next time get some," Vogel admonished her; "I've *done* my time in the missions."

Hazard heard the priest walk out into the hall and then stop as another set of steps came his way.

"Can I mooch a coupla smokes or a beer from you, pal?"

"Listen, don't get wise with me, Father," came the voice of Tommy Gruff, "or I'll knock you on your ass. Who the hell put you up to this crap? Some asshole?"

There next came the *thwack* of a slap on someone's face. "Step One," growled the voice of Father Vogel. "And now I am speaking to the demon inside you . . ."

Hazard stared. Poe's raven had just perched on his shoulder. Listening to the sounds of scuffling from the hall, he reflected on his introduction that morning to Zelig's selection as unit publicist, a grotesquely obese young woman who'd attempted to communicate with him in sign. Something from *The Satanist* was rubbing off: he was beginning to pay attention to omens.

He buzzed his secretary.

"Mr. Hazard?"

"Millie, get me Arthur Zelig, would you, please?"

When the call came, Zelig was in his office listening to a tape of *La Bohéme*. The mogul's bandages were gone, replaced by a *Phantom of the Opera* mask for which Zelig had given no explanation, although garlands of rumors had been tossed on the waters concerning a scheduled second operation and the mogul was frequently observed to be studying eight-by-ten head shots of Desi Arnaz.

The intercom buzzed.

"Yes, Muffy, my pet; what is it?"

"Jasnhazumnthree."

"Have him hold."

Zelig waited for the end of his favorite aria, the one by the slut, "Musetta's Waltz," then with a push of a button he stopped the tape. In the silence a thudding sharp rap was heard, Jules bumping his head against a wall. Zelig held still for a moment, listening. "That cabinet's knocking again," he said quietly. "It never used to happen 'til we started these spook films."

Zelig groped and found the speakerphone button.

"Yes, Jason?"

"Where's the script, Arthur? When can I see it?"

A quiet tension could be heard in Hazard's voice.

"Drood is working, don't worry," the mogul reassured him. "In fact, I just spoke to him, Jason. He called."

"How's it coming?"

"Does it matter to you, Jason?"

"Does it matter? We're making a movie."

"*My* movie."

"And my reputation, goddammit!"

"Drood told me it's the best he's ever done."

"Can I talk to him?"

"No, he's holed up somewhere."

"What's his number?"

"I didn't think to get it."

Silence. Then, "What page is he on?" asked Hazard tightly.

"What page?"

"Yes, how far is he along?"

"He didn't say."

"You didn't ask him?"

"No."

"Why the fuck is he taking so long? It's his book."

"Is there any need to raise your voice, Jason?"

"*Is* there?"

"Of course not. Drood is just having some problems."

"What kind?"

"Well, emotional problems."

"*What?*"

"Nothing serious."

"*Emotional* problems?"

"That's all."

"What *kind* of emotional problems?"

"I don't know," Zelig answered. "I just didn't think to ask. In the meantime no one's forcing you to do this, Jason. You can quit at any time and forget the three pictures."

Silence. Zelig heard only heavy breathing and hoisted a thumbs-up sign toward the tank. The snake, unused to the strange new mask, lay coiled in a corner on full alert. Something else was disturbing Jeff that day: Zelig had taken to calling him Toto.

"Shouldn't we be thinking of alternatives, Arthur?" came Hazard's voice in a strange, drugged monotone. "I could do the adaptation myself. "I'm fast. I could have it done in weeks."

"No, we've got to be faithful to the novel."

"I'd be faithful."

"No, you wouldn't. I know you. You'd wander."

"I've changed."

"But you're not what the audience wants."

"I'm not?" Hazard's voice held a tiny squeal.

"No, the people want Drood and the novel straight up. Here and there a few changes, of course."

The hairs on Hazard's voice stood on end.

"What changes?"

"Now you're shouting again."

"What *changes?*"

"Nothing big."

"Well, what are they? Are you sitting on the pages, you fuck? Have you got them already?"

"This is shameful."

"What *changes*, goddammit? Tell me *now!*"

"A slight shift in the character of the exorcists. They're no longer of the Jesuit order."

"Not Jesuits?"

"No."

"And that's it?"

"That's it."

"So what order are they going to be?"

"No order. They'll be rabbis who were formerly Beverly Hills plastic surgeons."

Zelig immediately disconnected, but not before hearing the beginning of the shriek.

CHAPTER TWO

"No, NOT JONATHAN DRUID—*Drood.*"

"Just a moment and I'll check with Registration."

Hazard clutched the phone with a white-knuckled hand. Almost lost in the branches of a huge potted ficus tree, his eyes demented and furtive, he was standing at a shelf of lobby telephones in the Akron Holiday Inn. A branch of the tree had brushed his face. He accepted a leaf in his mouth and started chewing.

"No, no Drood," said the operator, back on the line.

"He might be using some other name."

"What was that?"

The director spat out the leaf.

"He might be using some other name."

He consulted a list that he had scribbled on a piece of lined notepaper torn from a pad, pseudonyms used by the horror author on his earlier paperback bodice-rippers.

"Is there someone named Desmond Lash staying with you?"

"Oh, the author?"

"Yes, the author."

"No, I'd know if he was here."

She giggled.

"Irving Cutlass?" the director persisted.

"No, there's nobody here by that name, I'm quite certain."

"Laura Bierce?"

"Just a moment, I'll try to connect you."

The director's manic gaze flared wider, incredulous beacons in a deadpan face. He lifted a hand to bite on a fingernail and heard the tiny brittle crunching of his fate. Everything depended, now, upon Drood.

"The Hunt for Spooky Mr. October," as Tony DeSky had dubbed Hazard's quest, had started and ended at Infamous Artists, the agent not only for Hazard on *The Satanist*, but also for Jonathan Drood. "It's a package," DeSky had described it to Hazard with the usual globe-shaping gesture of his hands. "Now, you can't let on who told you," he'd cautioned at his Malibu home, where Hazard had tracked him down as the agent came in from a walk on the beach wearing shirt and tie, a banded boater and pinstriped trousers rolled up to his knees. "Okay, so now all of that's that and that's there," he'd gone on with compartmentalizing gestures. Lowering his head to sip at a beer, he had then rubbed sidewise at his lips with a finger, hunched forward and confided, "So now listen to this." Near the end of an exhausting thirty-city tour to promote *The Satanist*, the agent recounted, the author, while autographing copies of his novel in Akron, Ohio, the tour's last stop, was served with divorce and custody papers by a man who had stood in the line of fans and told Drood after serving him, "I love your work." In an action that was totally unexpected—the author until then had thought his marriage to be perfect—the suit demanded custody of Drood's two children in addition to one half of his total assets plus eighty thousand dollars per month in child support and for the care of half a dozen black cats. The reasons for the action, as alleged by Drood's wife, were that Drood had "ignored" her, did "nothing but write," and had forced her "on more than one occasion" to accompany the novelist on visits to cemeteries in the middle of the night "just to listen." ("To him?" she'd been asked in court. "No, not him." "Then to what?" "To *them*." "I see.") There was also an unspecified claim of "ill usage." Drood was emotionally annihilated. Blindsided and physically drained—the thirty-city tour had been done in thirty days, with the author submitting to an average of sixteen media interviews in each city—Drood, an unassuming, diffident soul, had holed up in his suite at the Akron hotel like some legendary mortally wounded bear.

"Is he writing?" the director had asked DeSky.

"Sure, he's writin'. He's doin' real good, I hear. He wants to take his mind off his personal problems so he's givin' it everything he's got. You should be happy."

Hazard told DeSky about Zelig's rabbis.

"Ah, that's crazy," the agent had retorted dismissively. "Zelig must be tryin' to get your goat."

"I don't know," Hazard ruminated then. "I don't know."

The director hadn't mentioned the rabbis to Sprightly.

"So what's goin' on in Akron?" she'd asked him with an interested frown when he told her of the trip.

"I've got to have a little talk with Jonathan Drood," he'd said lightly. "He's having a couple of problems."

"What kind?"

"Nothing serious," he'd shrugged. "Just domestic."

He missed the look that Sprightly had shot him.

"Jesus, give it up, would you?" she'd exploded. "Quit the project!"

"And walk out on a three-picture deal? Hey, come on!"

"Jason, how does that make me feel?"

"Whaddya mean?"

"Well, suppose some little genie appeared to you and she said to you, 'Hey, never mind, Sprightly, just fuck me and I'll get you a three-picture deal?' I've got to think in that scenario, pie, you'd get laid."

But Hazard had tuned out of her avowal early; his thoughts had banged to what he'd find in Drood's script. If it equaled the author's usual standard—or was even in the bat cave, Hazard had resolved—he would take Zelig's offer of new personnel; but if it fell short he would have to bow out: end of story and end of career.

The director examined the nail he'd just gnawed.

"Hello?"

Hazard started at the voice on the line: he'd expected Vincent Price or perhaps Darth Vader. But the voice that he'd heard was small and childlike; it sounded helpless and lost, forlorn.

"Jonathan?"

"You're not supposed to say that," said the voice.

"Is this Jonathan Drood?"

"Who's this?"

"Jason Hazard. I'm here in the lobby."

"I love your work," said the voice dispiritedly.

"Can I come up there to see you?"

"Come up?"

"Yes, is this a good time?"

"Oh, these are terrible times, Mr. Hazard."

"I mean is this a good time to come up and see you?"

"You mean fly here to Akron?"

"No—I'm in Akron right now. I'm in your hotel. I'm in the lobby."

"Are you mad at me or something?"

"Am I mad at you?"

"You sound kind of cross."

"No, I'm not at all cross. I'm just tired."

"Me too."

"What's your room number, Jonathan? I'd like to come up."

"Why?"

"I want to talk about the script."

"But we're talking."

"Yes, I know, but we need to talk more in depth, don't you think? I'm directing your baby, Jonathan. Don't you think we ought to have a meeting of the minds."

"Are you alone or by yourself?"

"I'm alone."

After getting the number of the author's room, Hazard rushed to an elevator, rode it upstairs, burst out of it the moment its doors began to open and then raced down the carpeted hall to Drood's door, where he stood and shook his head in renewed disbelief. The number of the room was 666.

Hazard rapped lightly with a knuckle.

"Who is it?" the author asked meekly.

"Jason Hazard."

"Who?"

"Jason Hazard. We just talked."

"Today?"

"Just now."

"I just wanted to be sure it was you."

"Yes, it's me."

"Nice to meet you, Mr. Hazard."

"Yes."

The director waited, but the door didn't open.

"Aren't you going to let me in?"

"I can't do that.

"But you said I could come up."

"Yes, I did, but I didn't say into the room."

Hazard scruted the door, looking frimmled.

"Now you know that I've come from California just to see you."

"I could stand at the peephole," Drood offered encouragingly. Then he added, "You might see my eye."

Hazard stifled a powerful impulse to scream. Instead he took another breath and found a sympathetic tone: "I'm so sorry about what's happened with the wife and kids."

"Wife and kids?"

"The divorce."

"What divorce, Mr. Hazard?"

"Yours."

"I've never been married, Mr. Hazard."

Holy shit, he's blocked it out!

Drood finished his statement:

"I'm alone."

Hazard heard a sound like a stifled whimper.

"Ah, Jonathan, they've hurt you pretty badly now, haven't they?"

"You don't know what they did to me, Mr. Hazard."

He's remembering, thought Hazard with a stab of hope.

"These people who hurt you—did they look like lawyers?"

"No. They were the people who asked me those imbecilic questions on all of those talk shows, Mr. Hazard. Do you know what it's like to do five hundred interviews with the cultural elite?"

"I have no idea."

"Well, it's hell, Mr. Hazard. It's absolute total hell on earth."

The director's eyes were beginning to shine.

"Do you think I might come in and sit down now, Jonathan?"

"They asked the same questions over and over, like, 'Why did you decide to write this book?' When I answered, 'Because that's what I do, I'm a writer,' they'd get real mad at me, Mr. Hazard. I kept trying to find the right answer and please them, but I guess I never did because they kept on asking it. I'm so tired, Mr. Hazard; really fozzed."

"I understand."

"They always asked me these three-part questions, with each part stupider than the other, like 'Where do you get your ideas for your books?' Then I'd answer one part but I'd be so wunched I'd forget what the other two questions were and not even try answering them at all. No one who was asking me the questions ever noticed, though. They weren't listening, Mr. Hazard."

"No, no one ever does listen, do they, Jonathan?"

"One man's *name* was Cultural Elite."

"Listen, don't you think—"

"In San Francisco once on TV they made me wear a big dirty old Mexican sombrero and say, 'We don't need no stinking badges.' Everyone who came on the show had to do it."

"Ah, Jonathan!"

"But New York was the worst," Drood moaned. His voice held a shiver of unspeakable dread. "This is where they hurt me really bad, Mr. Hazard."

"What happened in New York?"

"I can't tell you."

"But I'm really concerned."

"I can't tell you."

"You must."

A dense and extended silence ensued before Drood at last said miserably, "I appeared on the Letterman show with an owl that was dressed in a devil costume."

"Oh, well, that wasn't really so bad, was it, Jonathan? Okay, so the bird was dressed up in a devil suit. So what?"

"I wore one too."

The director's eyes were beginning to protrude. "Do you think I could come in now?" he emitted in a voice high-pitched from the strain of controlling hysteria. "I have to use the bathroom right away. Really, Jonathan."

"Things were really good for me once," Drood mourned. "I was happy. The world was at my feet. I met Elvis."

Hazard bowed his head into a hand and shook his head.

"I was staying at the Desert Inn in Las Vegas," Drood reminisced in his injured child's voice, "and someone in the lobby just walked right up to me and said to me, 'Elvis wants to meet you, how would you like to come up to his room?' Can you imagine? Elvis! He wanted to meet *me!* So I went up and I met him and his wife, Miss Priscilla, and he showed me a letter from President Nixon that he kept in a frame on his bedroom wall. Then he got out a whole bunch of books from somewhere, they were all about religion and philosophy and spirits, and a lot of it he'd underlined in ink and he stood there in the middle of the room nose-to-nose with me, reading me the underlined parts out loud. Then he changed his clothes and put on a kimono and he gave me a karate exhibition with his teacher. Elvis beat him up pretty badly, Mr. Hazard." The author paused and then said wistfully, "Those sure were pretty days. I think about that time I met Elvis quite a lot. But I don't know now." Drood's voice was forlorn again. "Maybe Elvis mistook me for someone else."

"No, he knew you were you!" Hazard rushed to assure him. "He was honored to meet you!"

"He was?"

"Oh, absolutely!"

"How do you know that, Mr. Hazard?"

"Elvis wrote to me about it."

"You met Elvis?"

"No, I wasn't important enough to meet him. He only wrote me letters."

"How come he wrote you letters?"

"He was answering my fan mail, Jonathan."

"Oh."

This seemed to satisfy Drood.

"Do you think we could talk about the screenplay?" Hazard lilted.

"Not a lot."

"Could I ask you one question about it?"

"I met Ryan O'Neal once," Drood reminisced.

"Oh, did you?"

"He was acting in a movie near my house. In the street. *Tough Guys Don't Dance* or something. I came out and I watched them for a couple of minutes. Mr. O'Neal had a severed woman's head in each hand; he was holding each one of them dangling by the hair, and before he did the scene he told some man, 'If this doesn't work, Norman, I'm hunting you down to the ends of the earth.' I thought that was an interesting thing to say."

"Only one little question on the script? Just one?"

"I'm so tired."

"Are the exorcists still Jesuits?"

"Yes."

Hazard almost collapsed against the door with relief.

"What made you think the exorcists weren't still Jesuits?"

"Oh, I don't know," Hazard said blithely. "Just a question."

"That would really be crazy," Drood muttered.

"I agree."

"That's the only change I *haven't* had to make."

Hazard lunged at the doorknob maniacally, rattling it frenziedly in hopes of an entry. It held. He stepped back from it and stared with wild eyes.

"Listen, Jonathan, let me in the room!"

"No, I can't."

"The story in the novel is *wonderful*, Jonathan! Why are you changing it around?"

"I'm the writer."

Hazard pounded on the door with his fist.

"Please don't do that," Drood whimpered.

"Who told you to change it, Jonathan?"

"My head hurts."

"Who told you to change it? Was it Zelig?"

"*He* told me."

"Zelig?"

"No, *he* did. Simpson."

"Who is Simpson?"

"My friend. He dictates the changes."

"He dictates?"

"He tells me what to write and I type it."

"In there?"

"Yes, in here."

"He's a writer?"

"Not basically."

"Then what is he?"

"I really can't tell you."

"Of course you can tell me; I'm your friend."

"No, you'd laugh at me."

"No."

"You'd think it's strange."

"You're the author of *The Satanist,* Jonathan—the rules that govern ordinary people cannot possibly apply to you!"

"They can't?"

"Not in twenty million years."

"Well, that's different."

"Who is Simpson?"

"He's this really big parrot, Mr. Hazard."

"Big parrot?"

"He's huge. He's invisible, too. You can't see him."

The director's eyes shone wildly, bulging, but he went on smoothly without hesitation, though his voice grew high and strained again as he asked, "May I read his pages, Jonathan?"

"I sent them all to Zelig. Don't you have them?"

"No, I don't," Hazard tried to say urbanely. "My wife and I were burglarized last week before I read them. The robber must be one of your fans, he took the pages. How many of them were there? Could you tell me that, Jonathan?"

"Eighty."

"Do you think you might spare me a copy?"

"In Portland once an interviewer asked if I could levitate."

"And what did you say to him, Jonathan?"

"Nothing."

"Was it part of a three-part question?"

"Yes."

"Could I have that other copy of the pages?"

"I'll go get them."

"Oh, thank you," said Hazard.

"Wait here."

The director's eyes bulged further. Then he heard an anomalous sound beyond the door that just might have been the squawk of a very large bird.

"Here it comes."

Drood's piping voice had returned.

Hazard happened to be staring down at the rug when a typed sheet of manuscript was slipped beneath the door. The director held his breath. "Is that the script?"

"Page one."

Another sheet appeared right above the first.

Hazard stared.

"Can't you open the door, please, Jonathan? I'd really like to have them all at once. Is that possible?"

"No, this way I can check them for typos as we go."

CHAPTER THREE

SPRIGHTLY PICKED HIM UP at the airport. Grimly, he got into the car, murmured, "Hi" and then fixedly stared straight ahead through the windshield. On his lap, tightly gripped, was a large brown file folder that he clung to as if for dear life.

"No kiss?" Sprightly frowned.

"Yeah, sure."

He leaned over and pecked her on the cheek distractedly, then returned to his rigid stare. A shuttle bus that whooshed in and parked in front of them with a gasp of pneumatic brakes was disgorging a band of Japanese tourists, disgruntled and dimly muttering and cursing that they hadn't met Spock or Captain Kirk and clutching rolled-up hundred-and-fifty-dollar Star Maps that somehow placed Graceland in Pasadena. Sprightly eyed her husband with concern. He seemed tense. She pulled the car out into traffic and then glanced at his lap.

"Is that it?"

"Is that what?"

"Is that the script?"

"Just the first eighty pages," he said without expression. He continued to stare straight ahead at the road.

"So?" she asked him.

"So what?"

"So how are they?" she demanded.

"I don't know. I haven't read them."

"You haven't *read* them?"

"No, I haven't."

"You didn't read them on the plane?"

"I'd like to savor them."

"But aren't you anxious?" she marveled.

"Not basically."

Driving into Malibu they passed Joey's Ribs. Sprightly grimaced. When they'd rented at the beach years back, they had savored Joey's ribs as perhaps the world's best, and most certainly the only decent meal within reach. This time when Sprightly dropped in there one day, she discovered that Joey's had acquired a new owner, a tall Pakistani with an eagle nose, trim black moustache and lilting accent. Sprightly asked him, "Have you changed the sauce recipe at all?" because she didn't want to order if they weren't the same. The Pakistani drew himself up, looking dumbfounded. "What? Change the sauce? What am I, a madman?" Faintly outraged, his black eyes gleamed with incredulity. "Why would I want to change this wonderful sauce?" he huffed. "Why in thunder did I *buy* this place, for God's sake!" Sprightly ordered the babybacks and took them home for dinner. The sauce proved disgusting; it had been totally changed.

"Joey's Ribs." Sprightly grimaced with distaste as they passed it.

" 'What am I, a madman?' " Hazard absently murmured.

They drove through the Malibu Colony guard gate, parked in the garage and entered the house. As she stepped inside, Sprightly paused and said, "Who changed the furniture around? I'm gone an hour and a half and the guy redecorates."

She called up the staircase,

"Hey, Ralph, what'd you do here? I liked it like it was!"

She looked down.

"No, it couldn't have been Ralph," she remembered. She walked to the open front door and shut it. "It must have been the day maid," Sprightly guessed. "Ralph went downtown to see a friend."

"Friends are good," said Hazard dully.

Sprightly glanced over at her husband. Shoulders slumped, he was standing at a mullioned bay window staring out at the ocean with clammy eyes. *Holy shit, he's got that Norman Maine look,* Sprightly fretted. And yet part of her hoped that the script was a disaster so that Hazard would be forced to abandon the film. *He's losing it. He's got to get off this picture.*

"You want to have a wine with me, pie? It's five o'clock."

Sprightly watched him. The director didn't move.

"No, I think I'll read the script," he intoned in a hollow voice that might easily have come from a coffin. "I'll just take it upstairs with me now and enjoy."

Sprightly eyed him with skepticism, then turned and walked away toward the kitchen. "I'll fix dinner."

His lips moved, murmuring inaudibly, "Be *silent* when you're speaking to me!"

He slouched to the foot of the staircase, turned wearily as one would to nod good-bye to Rochefoucauld, and then trudged with bent shoulders to the vaulted top-floor room that he used as his study and retreat. After shutting all the windows to block out the din of a misnamed sea, Hazard settled in a chair at a cedar desk and with a sigh drew the pages out of their folder. He'd been truthful; he really hadn't read them as yet. This was partly from reluctance to abandon all hope, although mainly from the dread of creating a disturbance reminiscent of the time a famed female lyricist with a phobic terror of heights had gone racing down the aisle of a DC–10 as it taxied for takeoff screaming over and over again, "Kill the priest!", an injunction that, in her case, unlike Hazard's, bore no relevance whatever to her life's situation or its manifestly altogether quite rich pageant.

Hazard stared dismally down at the title page. He felt cold, yet he reached for hope: many of the world's creative geniuses, he reflected, had been utterly mad, and not just temporarily like poor Drood. And yet it hadn't adversely affected their artistry; it might, in fact, have helped it. Hazard turned the page, read the words "Fade In" and thought: *So far he's done nothing wrong.*

Later, while Sprightly was busy preparing a pasta salad for their dinner, she heard an extraordinary sound from above. Earlier she'd heard a few other odd noises, but this one was different, more piercing, much louder. She set down an olive oil tin on the counter, rushed upstairs and burst into the study.

"Jason? Honey, what's going on? Is something wrong?"

"Nothing's wrong," said Hazard. Telephone in hand, he'd been dialing a number. He pressed on the disconnect bar. "Hiya, sweetie," he intoned in a strangely dead voice. It didn't go with the face. His eyes shone and seemed to be staring right through her and his lips were sickled up in a hideous grin.

"God Almighty, your face, pie! You look like death! Is it the script?"

"It's so powerful! It's blown me away!"

"Pie, you're kidding!"

"It's a miracle!" the strange voice uttered.

"Can I read it?"

She had moved to him, her eyes on the pages, but Hazard slapped a hand down on top of them protectively. "Not yet. It needs a teensy bit of a polish."

"Well, then, soon?"

"Hon, I've got to make this telephone call."

"Oh, okay."

She turned and started moving toward the stairs.

"Oh, well, at least I know the ending's really scary," she comforted herself. "My God, the way you screamed."

At his office, Arthur Zelig adjusted his mask and picked up the telephone. "Yes, Jason?" he purred. As he listened, the mask began to smile, a phenomenon observed in mask-face relationships of uncommonly lengthy duration and known as the Lord George Hell Effect.* The mogul pulled the telephone away from his ear and held it out toward the tank so that Jeff could more easily hear the demented raving and cursing. After that, without having said a word, he disconnected.

"Good news," Zelig hissed toward the tank. "Did you hear it? Hazard thinks the script is an abomination. He's threatening to show it to Bahamian Fred, who runs the bank that supplies us with our line of credit. But it's futile; back of Fred there is Credite Sleaze. In the meantime, I believe the trap's about to be sprung."

Back in Malibu, Hazard's hands were shaking. He looked down at the phone. His threat was empty: Years ago, when still under contract to Zelig, he'd complained to a friend on the board of

---

* After the hero of Max Beerbohm's "The Happy Hypocrite," who becomes his saintly mask.

directors that Zelig took advice from a snake named Jeff, but when the friend brought it up at a meeting of the board, at the end the chairman shrugged and said, "The snake gives us hits."

Hazard heard a distant rumble of thunder. He turned and looked out through a picture window at gray-blue clouds scudding low above the ocean. A sudden pelting rain made a clatter on the roof. Hazard rose up from his chair, found the stairs and descended like an animated rag under sentence of death-by-listening-to-rap. Sprightly, in the kitchen, was unable to see him as he walked somnambulistically out to the patio and climbed up the steps to the redwood deck overlooking the raging dung-dark sea where the waves were now pounding at the bulkheads savagely and thunder jolted and rattled while, across the way, near Catalina, lightning bullied the sky with webs of blinding white and flashes of blue, thus announcing, "This is no matte shot, assholes!" Suddenly the rain slashed down in torrents and thousands of horses and dogs raced for cover. In the west there was a crack in the clouds, a blush of rose. Hazard stared at it fixedly, it drew him. Was he really to be permanently barred from the candy store? he agonized. Must it be so? Searching his soul, he first emptied its pockets of its hollowest arguments and defenses: *Is this really such a sellout? Hell, it's only a movie. Can't I make it and forget it just like everybody else? Shit, man, everyone's entitled to a turkey. Why not me? Can't I have* my *aberration, my Devil's Gate, my flaming* Bonfire of the Insanities? *The public would forget it in time. But would I? Could I ever look Sprightly again in the face? Could I ever look* myself *again in the face? Jesus, what would* Elaine *think about it? Oh, my God!*

"Tell me what to do!" Hazard cried out aloud in a hoarse and anguished voice, half-crazed. The whited sea pounded madly at the bulkhead, and the waves and the rain engulfed his cry. "No one knows anything!" he shouted dementedly. "I don't know what to do! *You* tell me!"

The pink-tinted crack in the sky began to widen, and to Hazard's astonishment he thought he clearly heard, amid the lightning's play and the woofing thunder, a majestic voice that boomed commandingly:

"GIVE THE PEOPLE WHAT THEY WANT!"

It was Hazard's first truly religious experience.
It was also the Devil's Plan.

A month later, loudly whistling the theme from *Mr. Lucky*, a debonair man in the garb of a priest tripped lithely down the bullet-strewn, bloodstained steps of a lonely Manhattan subway station and antically loped to the edge of the platform. Uncannily resembling the late Robert Preston, he moved with the listing, cunning crouch of Professor Harold Hill in *The Music Man* and gripped a black valise. He stared down the tunnel and the lights, bright sentinels, that dwindled into darkness.

"Couldja help an old altar boy, Father? I'm a Cat'lic."

The man in black turned around to the derelict sitting on the ground with his hand held out, emaciated, toothless and dressed in rags. "Thank you for sharing that with me, friend," he replied with relentlessly slashing good cheer, and then added in a strong and rich, trained voice: "And now let me share a bit of *my* good news. Arthur Zelig has cast me as a lead in *The Satanist!* I'm playing Langhorne Desperé, the noted Jesuit philosopher-priest-composer!"

The bum looked confused.

"Father . . ." he faltered.

"Yes, I know it's overwhelming. I can see you brimming up. And now what of *your* good news? Tell me everything!"

"Father?"

The bum's eyes grew more fuddled.

"Ah, I see. Please allow me to introduce myself," said the man in the garb of a priest. From a pocket of his coat he extracted a business card and placed it in the bum's open hand. "I'm Emory Bunting, the noted actor," he announced. He pointed to the text on the card: "Also notice I'm a voice coach, drama coach and caterer. The number's on the bottom, should you need it; it's the service. In the meantime, could you possibly lend me a twenty until next Tuesday? I'm expecting an advance. Make it ten. No, I see it in your eyes—you hate the poor. Well, I make no judgment

upon you, friend, and as God is my witness I hold no grudge.
Father Langhorne Desperé will always keep you in his prayers."

A train had come roaring into the station. It stopped and pneumatic doors whooshed open. "And now I must be off, dear
friend," mourned Bunting. "Stay happy: it's the smiles that keep
us going."

As the derelict continued to gape with dazed eyes, Bunting
turned and did a skip-step into the subway car, then turned to
regard the bum, declaring fondly, as the doors of the car began to
close:

"I will always remember you this way."

*   *   *

It had begun. Zelig turned to the gleaming snake tank. "Ah, what a month it's been, hasn't it? My major casting has been completed and Hazard is in Malibu flowing with the tide. Shock treatment, Pavlovian conditioned response: when we turned the rabbis back into priests, he was so grateful he accepted dreadful actors in the parts. That's how they train directors in North Korea.

"So far, so good. We're rolling. When it's over I'll be cured of this awful blindness—it's useless, there's no money in it, Jeff, not a sou. And then that other nastiness that happened when she left—you know the one. Ah, Jeff, have you any idea, any inkling, of the utter depths of hell, the degradation, in knowing you're the only human alive with a penile implant that is impotent?

"Not for long, though. We shall overcome."

Part Six

GO NOT TO THE SET TODAY, CAESAR!

De hissibus non disputandum est.
—JEFF,
Latin for Snakes

CHAPTER ONE

ESTELLE BOOM, THE COSTUME designer, was measuring the length of Bunting's cassock in the wardrobe department of Zelig Studios. Principal photography was soon to begin.

"You know I spent a few years once preparing for the priesthood," said Bunting, "and Estelle, if nothing else, it did teach me one thing. Do you mind a little comment?"

"Go ahead."

"The suede loafers with the little brass bells?"

"What about them?"

"Are you sure that's authentic, my darling?"

"Absolutely. I did research. I called up a big religious goods store. It's in Hollywood."

"The Neon Chalice?"

"That's the one."

In the meantime, in an office next door to the shooting stage, Hazard was pacing with nervous energy and answering a question from Sally Quine, a pretty blonde reporter for People magazine. He wore blue jeans, white tennis shoes and a T-shirt. Now and then he'd tug at the bill of a baseball cap that all of the crew were wearing, black, with *The Satanist* in red above the brim. The director was passionate, driven, obsessed. Ever since receiving his heavenly voice-mail, there was always a ghost of a grin on his face, and, in his eyes, a perpetual feverish gleam.

"Poe and Mary Shelley," he fervidly expounded now, "would know *exactly* what it is that Drood is doing; they worked in that very same limbo, that elsewhere, between the supernatural world and this one. And yet even these echoes are just so much tapestry,

really, so much gilding of the central metaphor of the existential-
ist message: the terror of the lonely little candle flames of life set
adrift in the chilling, lightless sea of a cosmos seemingly devoid of
any meaning."

Quine looked up with a puzzled frown and pushed on the
bridge of her glasses with a finger. "You really find all of this
meaning in *The Satanist?*"

"Yes, and in abundance," Hazard said flatly. "It resonates with
Kierkegaard, Sartre and Camus. Stephen Hawking would compre-
hend that fully: *The Satanist* is boundless angst without edges."

"One more try!"

Franz Detritus had rushed in with two assistants who were

wheeling in a life-sized dummy on rollers that was dressed in the habit of a Catholic priest and, beside it, a squeaking metal cart that bore a mechanism and a canister of bile-colored fluid that connected to the dummy's interior via tubing. They had also rolled a large canvas screen into the room.

Hazard folded his arms and scrutinized the dummy with a steely and intensely judicious stare. "Go ahead," he said crisply, narrowing his eyes.

Detritus pressed a button. From the dummy's mouth the yellowish fluid spewed and vaulted projectilely onto the screen.

"Too much yellow," the director said gravely.

"That's what *I* thought," said Detritus. "Puke is greenish."

"Yes, it is."

"And the texture?"

"More oatmeal."

"Good eye, Jason."

"That's why I'm paid the big bucks."

The trio wheeled their mechanism out of the room.

Hazard loped to his desk and sat down in his chair. "Sorry for the interruption, Sally. You were saying?"

"Oh, well, I'd like to get on to something new."

"You've got it."

Hazard put his feet up on the desk, grinning madly and clasping his hands behind his head. Beneath the cap's shade his eyes glowed.

"Well, I've heard some rumors," remarked the reporter.

"Oh?"

"About funny things happening on the set."

"Funny things?"

"Paranormal phenomena. Weirdness."

"I'm surprised at you, Sally."

"So the rumors aren't true?"

"No, of course not."

"And I've also heard rumors of dissension on the set."

"Are you kidding me? Who told you that?"

"I really couldn't say."

The blind item had been placed, in fact, by Zelig, through his chief of publicity, Base Canard.

"Well, the rumor is bunk," sniffed Hazard. "Will we be much longer, incidentally? I'm expecting my wife here for lunch any second."

"Just a couple of questions on the script."

"Go ahead."

The director suddenly leaped to his feet, quickly picked up two thirty-pound dumbbells from his desk and rapidly curled them in front of the reporter. "I've got to stay in shape," he said. "A sound mind in a sound fucking body, correct? Directing is physically exhausting. I need this. Also I have enemies."

"Enemies?"

Quine was writing rapidly.

"Yes, enemies."

"Who?"

"If I knew would I be worried? Just write *enemies*."

"*Enemies*," murmured the reporter as she scribbled.

Hazard checked his watch. "One more question."

"Okay, about the script. Are you pleased with it?"

"I doubt we'll ever see its likes again."

"Jason, I'm worried sick about you. Look at you—look at your face," Sprightly fretted.

They were sitting at a table in the Zelig lot commissary. Hazard, whose appetite was usually spare, had consumed a Rod Steiger Double Sirloin, shrimp cocktail and a plate heaped with onion rings and fries. He stuffed a piece of raisin bread into his mouth. "My face?" Hazard asked her, chewing on the bread. He gripped her with his manic, fevered stare.

"Christ, you look like you're possessed."

"See the movie, read the book."

"That's not funny."

"I'm *fine!*"

"No, you're not fine at all."

"Not fine?"

"No, you're just not normal, Jason."

Sprightly watched without comment as Hazard shook pepper into his coffee.

"Hey, I'm always this high before shooting," he burbled.

"Jason, walk off this picture," she said to him urgently.

Hazard stirred the coffee, his grin demented. "And give up my three-picture deal? *Now* who's crazy?"

"Did you see what you were doing when we walked over here? You were stepping on every crack in the sidewalks. Do you know what that is? That's neurotic behavior."

He sipped at his coffee.

"Not *every* crack, Sprightly."

"How's your coffee taste?"

"Fine."

"You need a goddamn shrink."

"Just because I like the coffee? Babe, it's commissary coffee. It's not perfect."

"What's this 'babe' shit?"

"Is there nothing I can say that will please you?"

"Yes, Jason: you can say, 'I quit this picture.' "

"Honey, trust me; I know what I'm doing."

She folded her arms and looked away.

"Yeah, sure."

"We've just got to get through this," he insisted. "Look, I'll do a lot of things that will seem—well, unusual."

"Really?"

"And that's when I'll need you the most. I need your trust. Have I got it?"

"Oh, don't be so ridiculous. *Please!*"

"Honey, look at me."

She turned her head and scrutinized him sidewise. "I'm looking."

"Have I got your total trust and your loyalty?"

"What the hell kind of shit is this?" she wondered.

"Have I got it? You would never walk out on the picture?"

"*Me* walk?"

He had taken her hand in both of his. Now he squeezed it. "You promise?"

"*Pie, you're hurting my hand!*"

"Do you promise me, sweetheart?"

"I *promise!*"

With a sigh he released her hand and she shook it to restore the circulation. "God, your *grip!*"

"Can I sell some dessert here, folks?"

Their waitress stood by. She sounded and looked like Bea Arthur. "Anything?"

Sprightly shook her head. "No, not for me."

Hazard grabbed the dessert card and rapidly read it. The manic grin and stare were back.

"What's this *Coming to America* Sundae?" he asked.

"Oh, that's a great one," the waitress said dryly. "It's super-big gobs of five flavors of ice cream served in a great huge half-gallon bowl and over it mocha fudge sauce, crumbled brownie, peaches, cherries and tons of nuts and then slathers and slathers of fresh whipped cream. You don't eat it, though, we just let you look at it awhile, then we pick it up and take the whole thing back inside. It's some kind of a diet thing: it's got fat and tons of goodies and calories and stuff but it somehow ends up a loss."

"You're kidding."

"Yeah, I'm kidding. You want one? They're good."

"Yeah, bring it," said Hazard.

"Comin' up."

She slewed away toward the kitchen.

"Honey, when do I get to see the script?" asked Sprightly. "It's all finished now, right? It's all done?"

"Yes, it's totally finished and proofed."

"And so when do I get it?"

"Get it?" He stared at her blankly.

"Pie, we're starting on Monday; I mean, rehearsalwise. Remember? I've got to have a script."

"No rehearsal," he corrected. "We're shooting."

"No rehearsal?"

"No, this film demands total spontaneity. That's one of the reasons I've been guarding the script. I've had everyone working from the novel and my notes. As for cast, every morning you'll be given that day's pages."

"Are you kidding me?"

"I got the idea from Richard Brooks. That's exactly what he did when he shot *In Cold Blood*. He said he didn't want the actors playing the entire script in every scene. You understand?"

"Oh, well, sort of."

"We'll rehearse as we shoot."

He fished out a credit card and placed it on the table.

"Jason, what was that mule doing parked outside the stage?"

"What mule?"

"Mr. Guy, the Talking Mule. I saw his trailer, it was parked by the stage."

"I didn't see him."

"Well, he's there. I just wondered."

"Sure."

Zelig turned off the secret intercom linking him to every foot of space on Stage Eleven. The sounds of construction had warmed his heart. "It's all happening, Toto," he rasped. "It's come to pass. Now she'll see what he's made of, this fool, Jason Hazard: how selfish and ego-driven he is; how shallow and corruptible; how venal; how not yare. She will see him as he grovels and shamelessly prostitutes himself; worse, prostitutes her as well. And for what? For more chances at self-exhibition."

Zelig scratched the nose of his new Candice Bergen mask. "It's a character issue," he concluded: "that is the heart and soul of the

Plan. He will show himself unworthy of her and she will leave him. In the end she will come back to me. That fool! He'll have nothing but ashes when this is all over! Do you think there'll be an audience of even ten people for those three films that I've agreed to let him make when he's known to all the world as the director who managed to destroy the invincibly indestructible, the greatest motion-picture material in years? In the meantime, if I know her she may leave him even sooner. I expect her to be calling me almost any day. Just wait until she gets her first peek at that script."

The snake shuddered. Zelig had read him the pages.

CHAPTER TWO

HAZARD PUSHED IN THE air with his hands toward a wall of the Georgetown bedroom set. "We'll be shooting in that direction, Smoke," he said. "Go on and light it and we'll start with the master."

Today was the beginning of principal photography. Two scenes had been scheduled to be shot, and the assistant director had padded to the dressing rooms of the actors, handing out scenes. "Your pages," he had whispered to Sir John Tremaine, the noted British Shakespearean actor who'd been cast as a Catholic bishop in Georgetown. "Oh, how terribly thoughtful," Tremaine had said drily. "Rather an intriguing procedure, this. Of course, it would never have occurred to me at all that I might be provided with the words I was to speak. How very useful. Had that ever occurred to you as well?"

"I'm not sure what you're saying, Sir John."

"No."

Emory Bunting had been next. In spite of the director's heated opposition, Zelig had insisted upon an unknown: "You want Paul Newman coming in with all his baggage? People would be saying, 'Hey, Newman looks great,' or 'What a wonderful actor' instead of just losing themselves in the story. But an Emory Bunting; ah, that's something else. Emory Bunting *is* Langhorne Desperé."

"Here you are, sir: Father Langhorne Desperé, Scene one hundred seven."

"Bless your heart, son. I'll remember you tonight at Morton's as we bow our heads in communal prayer at the Jerry and Helen Weintraub table."

At the time of her reception of the long-awaited pages, Sprightly was locked in the lotus position while Ralph tried to pacify her anxiety as to what they might contain.

"Breathe in deeply and altogether totally relaxing while all the time thinking of goodness and dullness," the guru instructed Sprightly in a drone, "and then afterward breathing out all evil poo-poos."

Hazard's light rapping at the door interrupted them. He stepped in and announced, "Scene Two," his eyes wild and crafty and with pinpoint pupils, like those of a deeply psychotic fox.

"About time," grumbled Sprightly. She reached out and snatched the pages from his hand with a rustle. Ralph quietly slipped into the hall and ommed away.

Hazard grasped the doorknob and pointed to the hallway. "I'll be standing right outside," he told Sprightly unreadably.

"Right."

She turned away, put the pages down in front of her makeup mirror, hunched over them and started to read.

"Right outside," repeated Hazard in that same dead monotone. He was motionless, staring at Sprightly; then he stepped outside, closed the door and waited with folded arms and a lowered head.

The first thing Hazard noticed in the minutes thereafter were the tendrils of either smoke or ectoplasm that were curling up from under the door. After that he heard a sighing sound, he thought, like a ghostly whimper or lament, and then it seemed that the door and the floor were trembling. The director kept his head down, nodding it slightly, the sadistic surgeon in the movie *King's Row* brooding quietly, "Yes, it is exactly as I thought."

"JASSOONNNNNNNNNNN!"

Before the piercing shriek had ended the director had adroitly slipped into the room, his expression as wide-eyed and mad as before. Sprightly was standing by the mirror staring at him with incredulous, popping eyes. She took a step forward. "You crazy fuck!" she cried and then whapped him in the face with the pages. "What in the hell do you think you're doing? Have you lost it? Are you really going to film this shit?"

"We must."

She hit him again. "We must *not!* Is this a joke? Jason, where are the pages, the real ones?"

"Please lower your voice."

"Here, it's lower," she gritted in a whisper. "Now where are the fucking real pages?"

"These are they."

"*These are* they?" Her voice squealed and was rising. "*These are* they? No, *these* are they!" she erupted in a squall as she slapped him again in the face with the pages. "They're disgusting and obscene and a goddamn travesty! You're telling me Jonathan Drood wrote this shit?"

"He transmitted them."

"*Transmitted them?*" Her darting eyes appraised him with alarm: his grin, his mad stare, his fevered brow. "Jason, go and see a shrink, would you, please? Would you see one?"

"What's the problem?"

"Jason, *that* is the problem, that *question!* Can't you see they'll make a citizen's arrest on this movie? It's just vile and you can't fucking do it!"

"Well, we're doing it."

She flung away the pages. "No way!"

"But you promised!"

"Are you shooting up, Jason? Are you drugging? Are you putting some Peruvian shit in your Slice?"

"*You promised!*" he suddenly roared.

It quelled her.

She turned and flopped down on her makeup stool, and then lowered her head into her hands.

"Sir John's going along with this, Jason?"

"He's a total professional."

She flipped him the bird.

"This is not what Gautama instructed," he said gravely.

She lowered her face back into her hands.

The director came over and knelt beside her, put his arm around her shoulder and kissed her brow. She looked up with despair and adoration in her eyes. "Oh, my God, you're so sick, pie. Sick. So sick."

For a moment the manic grin disappeared as he exhorted,

"Look, I'm not the one who wrote this dicking movie and I'm not the one who's spending forty million to make it. I told you, this is something we just have to get through. After that it's easy riding: I'll have my three pictures and I'll make them all forget this piece of crap. I'll do it, I'll make you proud!"

She looked at him dreamily and fondly.

"You promised!" he said urgently. "You *promised!*"

"I was just thinking of something," she mused. "You remember that time when you walked through the toughest turf in Harlem with a boombox on your shoulder at maximum volume blasting Beethoven's Fifth?"

She searched his eyes. They held no memory.

"Honey, will you do it?" he pleaded.

She looked down and mutely nodded. "Yeah, I promised."

Overjoyed, Hazard hugged her. "God, I love you!" he effused. "I just love you!"

She looked over at the pages on the floor.

That night the famed couple lay awake in bed with their backs to one another and at maximum distance. Beginning with the end of the day's last shot, Sprightly'd wrapped a shawl of ice around her shoulders and was distant, uttering no more than the barest civilities. Now both of them listened to the surf as it pounded and rattled great shudders through the wood-frame house.

"Sprightly?"

The word broke a half-hour's silence.

"Sprightly? You awake?"

"I'm not speaking to you!"

A tight-lipped minute ticked by. Then Sprightly asked sharply with her eyes closed, "What is it?"

"Do you ever hear voices in the water?"

Sprightly's eyes opened, rigidly staring. Hazard's voice sounded childlike and worried. She said, "What?"

"Do you ever hear voices in the waves?"

"No, Jason."

"Are you sure?"

"Yes, I'm terribly sure. But you hear them?"

"Yes, I do. I hear them saying my name."

"All the time?"

"No, sometimes they say *Fuck you.*"

"What I mean is do you hear the *voices* all of the time?"

"Just near the ocean." His tone remained worried and dis-tracted. "Like now. They're saying *Jason.* Can you hear it?"

"No, I can't."

"Well, just listen."

Sprightly's eyes were still wide with alarmed surmise. She waited, then said hollowly, "No, I don't hear them."

"It happens when the wave hits the bulkhead."

"Oh, is *that* it?"

"Do you ever hear rapping sounds, Sprightly?"

She turned over and goggled at his back.

"At the door?"

"No, in the house. I hear knocks. It's like a code."

"Oh, I see."

She propped her head up on an elbow. "So how long has this been happening, sweetie?" she asked him, straining to sound nonchalant and undisturbed.

"About a month," he responded bleakly.

"That long?"

"Ever since I came back from Akron."

"Any other funny things going on?"

"Well, the telephone."

"The telephone, sweetheart?"

"Yes. The other night it was ringing in my study."

"Don't you like it when it rings in your study?"

"Before I could answer," he continued in that worried, dead voice, "the receiver floated up off the cradle."

Sprightly's eyes widened further.

"Jason, who was on the line?"

"There wasn't anyone."

She quietly sighed in relief and closed her eyes.

"Jason, think about the shrink, would you, please?"

"Yes, I'm thinking."

"Okay."

She rolled over again and pulled at bedding when her eye caught a glow near the base of the floor. "Does any of this have anything to do," she asked with that falsetto of strain creeping back, "with your putting all these nightlights all over the house?"

"Well, we need them."

"Dozens of them?"

"Yes. It's too dark. I can't even find my way to the bathroom."

From somewhere in the house Ralph's quiet voice drifted up to him faintly: "Beginning of wisdom."

Hazard paid no mind. It was just another voice.

An hour later the director was still awake. He got up out of bed and padded down to the kitchen where he made himself a mug of hot chocolate with milk. Ten minutes later he returned upstairs with the look of a man who has seen a vision that is singularly lacking in any good news. Standing by the bed with shell-shocked eyes, he croaked huskily, "Sprightly! Sprightly, you awake?"

She turned her head, rubbed her eye with a knuckle and squinted. "Yeah, I guess I am now. What's up?"

"It's Barbra!"

She turned on a bedside lamp, then bolted upright. "Oh, my God, that look on your face! Pie, what is it?"

He recounted that while drinking his cocoa in the kitchen he had heard a meow, looked around and seen Barbra in the act of performing the Purina cat's cha-cha step, which sufficiently thought-provoking act she had followed by expanding to twice her normal size and then emitting a venomous, guttural snarl.

Sprightly lowered her forehead into a hand.

"Ah, holy shit," she murmured long-sufferingly.

"Then I think she was—"

"Jason, that's enough!" Sprightly quelled him, snapping her head up with flashing eyes. "You are seeing a shrink, do you understand me? You are seeing one as soon as you possibly can!"

"But I saw it!"

"See a shrink or I'm walking the picture!"

"Okay! Just don't yell. You just blotted out a really loud voice in the ocean."

Her face went back down to her hand.

"Holy shit!"

He said, "It could have been something important."

Late at night in her Studio City apartment, Ann Warner, the script supervisor on the picture, was meticulously working at her daily chore of memorializing scenes as they had actually been rendered, as compared to the original plan of the script. Each numbered take bore an explanation of what the director had chosen to be printed, plus notes on how the dialogue and action might have varied:

Take Two, 75 mm, MASTER; n.g., camera. . . . Take 7, 50 mm, pan from Blessing to figure under covers of bed. Good timing. Director liked best.

The supervisor sipped at a cup of coffee mercifully laced with her favorite scotch. Stunned, still in shock since reading the scenes, she'd made numberless typing errors this night. Setting down the mug, a gift of Telly Savalas—it said, "Who loves ya, baby?" on the front—she rubbed at the corners of her eyes with thumb and finger and then picked up the pages to proof them yet again:

SC. 2–2A:
Int. Bedroom in Georgetown House—Night. Dressed in a slip, Ellen Blessing lays atop her bed. She wears reading glasses and is talking into a telephone. In her hand is what appears to be a script that is bent back and opened at an early page.

Ellen Yeah, what scene are we starting with tomorrow? Scene Twenty? *(listens briefly)* Yeah, I thought so. *(listens)* No, he's sleeping. Can it wait until morning? *(listens)* Yeah, I got it. I'll tell him first thing, okay? Goodnight.

She hangs up the telephone, sets down the script, sits up, steps into her fluffy slippers, then rises and walks toward door. The CAMERA FOLLOWS her into the HALL and from there into:

Int. Small Bedroom in Georgetown House—Night. A bed. A figure beneath the blankets. Ellen shivers, as if from cold; spots an open window, moves to it, shuts it, then turns and stares fondly at the figure in the bed. She folds her arms and moves closer. We now can discern two equine ears protruding from the covers.

Ellen I sure do love you, Guy.

From under the blanket, a gentle whinny. Ellen adjusts the covers, leaves room.

Take 1, *incomplete: after whinny, actress rushes at camera, screaming.*

Take 2, *print. Ears partially hidden, but director wants to move on.*

SC. 107:
Int. Catholic Bishop's Office—Day. A long oval conference table. Sitting opposite one another are the The Bishop and Fr. Langhorne Desperé. The Bishop absently strokes an angora cat that is languidly sprawled across his lap. Open on

the table before him is a copy of the Catholic *Roman Ritual* (N.B., Props: the *larger* edition). The Bishop's dry wit spawns subtle double-meanings that tend to sail over the blunt priest's head.

THE BISHOP So. You are here to obtain my permission for performance of an exorcism on a mule. Does that sum it up fairly, Father Desperé?

DESPERÉ Yes.

THE BISHOP And it's not some sort of metaphor, Father? It's an actual mule?

DESPERÉ I'm pretty sure of it, Your Grace.

THE BISHOP How very odd.

DESPERÉ Well, you see, it's not an ordinary mule.

THE BISHOP I well imagine.

DESPERÉ It's the famous Mr. Guy.

THE BISHOP Mr. Guy?

DESPERÉ Mr. Guy, the Talking Mule. He's in the movies.

THE BISHOP Oh, no doubt!

DESPERÉ He's here in Georgetown filming *Mr. Guy Meets Congress.* Mrs. Blessing—she's the owner of the mule, Your Grace— she's extremely distraught and begs our help.

THE BISHOP (*stroking the cat*) And you would want to do the exorcism personally, Father?

DESPERÉ Yes, I feel I'm highly qualified, Your Grace. I know the way the mule thinks.

THE BISHOP God knows you do. And yet we must be very careful in this matter, must we not? For should the case involve no more than some mental illness, the ritual of exorcism itself might either strengthen or *implant* the delusion of possession. You're convinced this case is genuine, Father Desperé?

DESPERÉ Well, it seems to fit most of the accepted criteria, Your Grace.

THE BISHOP Ah, but does it, now, Father? Does it?

The Bishop dons wire-frame reading glasses and is searching the text of the book.

THE BISHOP (CONT'NG) The *Roman Ritual* demands that the—
Yes—yes, here it is. *(reading aloud:)* ". . . that the case be attended by unambiguous and verifiable paranormal phenomena." *(removes glasses; looks up at Desperé)* You are certain these
are present in this case, are you, Father?

DESPERÉ Well, the mule has been speaking in an unknown
tongue.

THE BISHOP Yes, I daresay he has.

Take *1: n.g., camera.*

TAKE *2: n.g., Bunting goes up on lines.*
TAKE *3, n.g., same as 2.*
TAKE *4, n.g., same as 2.*
TAKE *5, n.g., same as—*

Warner looked up. She'd had enough. She glanced at the next
day's breakdown of scenes.

Language expert discusses tape of possible "unknown language" sample received from Fr. Langhorne Desperé for
analysis. Language expert plays tape backwards: it's English—1940s Andrews Sisters recording of "Rum 'n Coca-
Cola."

Warner's eyes glazed over and then she closed them and lowered her disbelieving head to the typewriter.

"Christ!"

Suddenly she looked up and glanced around.

She thought she'd heard somebody calling her name.

CHAPTER THREE

"Do you find that you enjoy taking risks, Mr. Hazard?"

The psychiatrist, a sunny-minded man who wore sandals and was named Dr. Isadore Mindlin Shriek, was on the staff of a holistic medical center on Madonna Drive in Venice Beach. Hazard had been seeing him for double and triple sessions each night for the past three weeks.

"Why?"

"Well, your name," explained Shriek.

"I was born with my name."

"But you didn't choose to change it, now, did you? Just something to think about, that's all. In the meantime, I've now read the *Satanist* script, and of course I find it's written on a number of levels, though the central theme, to my mind, is quite clear: it's all about illusion versus reality. Is that anywhere close to how you see it?"

"On the button."

"Incidentally, what's your profit participation?"

"Six percent of the gross," answered Hazard.

"And is that rolling gross or pure?"

"It starts at two-and-a-half-times negative cost."

"Ah, I doubt you're going to see very much out of that. The mass audience won't get it."

"No, probably not."

"Now then, any more projections? Hallucinations?"

"No."

"No more voices? No problems with the cat?"

"None at all."

"You understand what was happening to you, don't you? Under stress you projected into your environment the thing that was utterly consuming you, your vision of the meaning of the film. And what was that?"

"Illusion versus reality."

"I expect you'll be fine from now on."

This sanguine prediction held true for two days. On day three, while Hazard was lunching in his office, a short, grinning man in flamenco attire clomped in, stomped his boots and cried out, "Olé!" with a quick, curling flourish of his hands above his head.

Hazard stared.

The man's grin fell apart. "Too much?"

"Who are you?"

"I'm Dwayne Mateen, the choreographer. That sequence you're adding is smashing, by the way. *Quelle* concept! Dancing exorcists and demons! Love it!"

In an instant, eighty hours of psychiatry were dust.

By the end of a stupefying, desperate day, the director's manic

look had returned to full Harpo. In addition to the blast of the musical sequence, a problem of temperament had sprouted. Asked to make the actors' breaths come frosty during the exorcism of the mule, Franz Detritus had designed, and caused to be built, a refrigerated duplicate bedroom set which Guy, for some reason, refused to enter, so that much of the day had been spent in attempting to feed him sedation-injected carrots—Guy also had a morbid fear of shots—and then attempting to lure him into the set with oat croissants and lumps of sugar; but nothing had been able to calm Guy's terrors, with the consequence of bridling, bucking and braying, plus copious effluxions all over the stage, although, to Guy's credit, no one heard him place blame. At five a shaken Hazard called a wrap on his day and left the effects crew to sort out the problem. En route home, he'd been detoured around to the Valley because of a slide on the Pacific Coast Highway and he made the long drive to Malibu Canyon and thence to the beach in a state of somnambulism, his eyes fixed numbly ahead while his lips kept mouthing in a soundless litany of horror, again and again, "Dwayne Mateen!"

The director walked into the house to find darkness. Sprightly wasn't scheduled to work that day and she'd driven to the Springs with Ralph to get away and to pick up some dates "in remembrance of Floyd." Hazard reached around to the living room wall, groped, found a switch and turned on the lights. From the beachside blackness of a moonless night, he heard the draggy, crackling ebbing of a rock-crammed surf. As he looked around and took off his *Satanist* cap—he'd started wearing it again around four o'clock—the living room and entry hall lights dimmed down, flickered eerily, and plunged into spooky darkness.

The director stood frozen by the staircase. *Thank God for my nightlights*, he fatuously thought as he saw that, mysteriously, they still glowed.

Then he heard something.

Singing. Barbra Streisand. Upstairs.

He looked up and called, "Sweetheart? You there?"

No response. He thought Sprightly might have turned on her bathroom radio, or was playing a recorded tape; then he realized with a prickling down the back of his neck that the singing was totally unaccompanied. He frowned in consternation. He knew that Barbra Streisand owned a home down the beach, and for an instant the deranged thought flashed through his head that Streisand had broken into the house. He lowered his face into a hand and shook his head. *Bananas. I am losing it altogether.*

He looked up again, cocking an ear, amazed. *Shit, that is Streisand! It's her! She's in the house!* Was she visiting Sprightly? he wondered in astonishment. Had she given her a home demo tape? They might have met at the exercise parlor down the road. Mesmerized, he walked up the creaking stairs, following the singing to the second-floor landing and then into his bedroom where he turned on a light. Moments later he was bolting from the room in a panic. He rushed down the steps and almost ran into Sprightly and Ralph as they were entering through the front door weighed down with bags of fruit from the Springs.

"Holy shit, am I glad that you're here!" Hazard panted.

Sprightly frowned in alarm. "What's wrong?"

"You won't believe it! Feel my heart, it's still pounding!"

"Ralph, turn on the lights!" Sprightly ordered.

"You can't! They turned off on their own!" Hazard blurted.

Ralph's finger hit a switch and the lights came on.

Sprightly eyed Hazard with a dawning hopelessness.

"Is this starting all over again? Fifty nightlights and your heart still goes boom-pitty-boom just because you couldn't turn on the living room lights?"

Hazard's stare became faraway and empty, like an alien pod's in *The Invasion of the Body Snatchers* masquerading as a cop in some village. "You don't know what I saw up there," he uttered hollowly. He pointed back over his shoulder.

"Your cat! She was singing like Barbra Streisand!"

"*What?*"

"Swear to God! She was singing 'My Man'!"

Sprightly sagged in despair to the arm of a sofa. "How much have we paid this psychiatrist?" she groaned.

"Sweetheart—Barbra *is* Barbra Streisand!"

After Hazard had been heavily cocoaed and bedded, Sprightly made an urgent call to Isadore Shriek but got only his answering machine, which held the message, "I will call you as soon as I'm back from Tahoe. Don't panic: shit happens. Whatever it is, it won't kill you."

The next furious call that she made was to Zelig.

"Hello, Arthur, you weasel-faced, plastic-dicked fuck. This is me, your little pissed-off exxie, Sprightly. Yeah, yeah, yeah, never mind all the greetings, you shithead. I want you to fire my husband off this picture. Would you, please? Would you let the poor son of a bitch go?"

Far away, in his fog-enshrouded Bel Air mansion, Zelig, in his study, turned his head toward Miss Peltz, who was seated beside him on a couch. She'd been reading *Variety* to him aloud. He reached out and excitedly squeezed her thigh as his lips formed the words *It's her! It's her!*

"What an odd request," he then purred into the telephone. "Are you serious about this, cupcake?"

"I am begging you, Arthur, you prick! Let him go!"

"Is it usual for beggars' petitions to the king to commence, *You prick*," Zelig asked urbanely, "or am I right in assuming that it's rather poor form?"

"Alright, I'm sorry! I take it all back! Just let him go!"

"Well, there *could* be a mode of salvation for Hazard."

"What is it? I'll do anything, Arthur! Just tell me!"

"Come back to me, precious."

"*What?*"

"Come back."

"Are you crazy?" Sprightly shouted.

"There is no other way," Zelig rasped into the phone. "If you loved him you'd come back to me so that I would free him. That would be true love, Sprightly: the truest."

"You've done all of this deliberately, you miserable asshole?"

"Come back."

"Fuck you and the spaceship you landed in!"

"I'll pretend I didn't hear that, gumdrop."

"Do you want me to say it again?"

"Look, I'm flexible. I'm willing to negotiate. Perhaps even one tender night of love with you would serve to put an end to this curse upon my eyes, this awful blindness."

"*What?*"

"It might even prove a cure for the plastic."

She slammed down the phone with a shattering force.

Livid, she walked out to the deck and breathed deeply, then finally came back in, refreshed. She went up to the bedroom and stood by the bed. "Jason?" she cautiously whispered. When no answer came, she felt relieved. She turned around and walked into their wardrobe closet where Barbra lay asnooze in her favorite niche, a snug corner under Sprightly's full-length mink coat.

"Barbra?"

The cat weakly mewled and looked up, then returned to her dream of disembodied grins.

"Babs, you're getting too fat," Sprightly murmured dispiritedly. "Tomorrow I put you on a diet."

Barbra's silence was not to be construed as consent.

Sprightly got undressed, slipped softly into bed and in an hour fell asleep with a desperate heart.

Shortly after dawn on the following morning, the actress sipped orange juice, deep in thought, while ignoring the yogurt and dates set before her. "Eat, Missy," Ralph nagged her from a seat across the table. Suddenly a clattering was heard on the stairs as Hazard descended cheerily humming, his brown leather briefcase bobbing in his grip. He stopped by the table, ajangle. The feverish, manic grin and stare that had vanished in the doings of the night had returned. "Hi, gang! What a sleep I had! Super night! Say, is this a great life at the beach or what! Gentle surf; it's like a lullaby at night, it's Brahms. Ralph, get out of that position, old sport, you'll cramp." Sprightly eyed him from underneath hooded lids, then blenched as her doomed gaze fell to the briefcase and she wondered what horror it contained for this day.

"Can we talk about Barbra?" she asked him tonelessly.

"What about her?"

"Last night."

"Last night?"

Her gaze flicked up to him.

"You don't remember?"

"Not really. Say, remind me to stop in at Joey's tonight and pick up a whole mess of those fabulous ribs."

*   *   *

At approximately 9:48 that morning, the difficult lighting had been completed on a massive composite photo backing of a wooded area of Georgetown down by the C&O Canal. Zelig, with a history of "improvophobia," had refused to permit location work "in the interest of filmic challenge," although it had also been bruited about that the Georgetown Community Citizens' Council had a member who not only had Egyptian parents but had even played bridge once with Omar Sharif. "We'll build fucking Georgetown on the studio lot!" the mogul had ranted at the tank in his office. Jeff, who hadn't dropped from a tree just yesterday, knew that the subject was potentially explosive and pretended to be lost in coiled sleep.

"Miss God? We're all ready for you now on the set."

The second assistant director was rapping on Sprightly's dressing room door. The pages of the script had been handed out earlier and Emory Bunting was already on the set.

"Ready for rehearsal," the assistant finished.

"I'm not coming," said Sprightly in a quiet voice. It was difficult to gauge its texture and mood.

"You're not coming to the set, Miss God?"

"No, I'm not."

The assistant heard the sound of a drink being stirred. He leaned in closer, angling his head. The antenna of his walkie-talkie unit scraped the door. "Can you tell me when you think you'll be coming, Miss God?"

"No, I don't think so."

"Are you coming at all?"

"Never ever."

Jason Hazard had come up. "What's the holdup?"

"She says she's not going to come out, Mr. Hazard."

"She's not coming?"

"Never ever."

"Lenny, when did you give her the pages?"

"First thing."

Hazard gestured with a thumb. "Go on, Lenny, do some work with the extras. I'll take care of this."

The assistant mutely nodded and left.

Hazard tried the dressing room door. It was locked. He rapped lightly. "Sweetheart? It's me. Open up."

"I've been candid with you all of my life."

"How many drinks have you had, my angel?"

"Not enough."

Hazard heard the gug of liquor over ice. His manic stare and fixed grin remained frozen and vivid, but his eyes, in a possibly alarming development, had taken to rolling like a cartoon wolf's.

"Let me in."

"I'm not doing this scene today, Jason."

"I knew you might say that, sweetheart."

"You knew it?"

"Just trust me. The events in this script aren't literal."

"They aren't?"

Hazard's eyes became particularly shiny and desperate: Sprightly was sounding like Jonathan Drood.

"This is allegory, sweetheart, fantasy—truth that's wrapped up in a big ball of myth. Don't you see? The more wild the hyperbole we use, the more vividly the symbolism's going to stand out!"

"I've been thinking," said Sprightly in a sad, quiet voice.

"Thinking what?"

"I'm thinking maybe you'd be better off without me."

"Honey, stop talking nonsense. We've already established you."

Instantly the dressing room door flew open and Sprightly stood framed there, drawn up like Joan Crawford, haughty and livid with her nostrils narrowed and her eyes bulging totally out of her head. In costume, she was wearing a colorful babushka with multiple "Winterhaven, Florida" inscriptions tastefully dispersed in its checkered design.

"You are vile!" she said icily. "Absolute scum!"

She swept past him and then onto a parklike set where she slipped on her oversized pair of dark glasses and then turned and looked grimly at Bunting beside her. He leaned in his head, looking mildly puzzled and bemused, and asked quietly, "Are we really going to do this?"

She nodded.

"Okay, quiet on the set!" the assistant director called out. "Hold the hammering! Quiet for rehearsal!"

Just before Hazard was to call out "Action," Sprightly turned to him and silently mouthed, "You disgust me!"

That night, Ann Warner grubbed at her notes:

SC. 57A:
EXT. C&O CANAL AREA—DAY. Desperé and Ellen Blessing walk slowly along the canal. From time to time Ellen drags nervously on a cigarette. Desperé is studying her intently. As she speaks she avoids his gaze.

ELLEN How do you go about getting an exorcism, Father?
DESPERÉ Are you kidding me?
ELLEN What if someone—very close to you turned out to be—possessed?
DESPERÉ (bemused) Well, I'd sit down and have a talk with him; show him some sense.
ELLEN No, I mean it!
DESPERÉ Sure, you mean it.
ELLEN (shrieking) For God's sake, Father! It's my ass!

TAKE 1: 50 mm, front tracking; n.g., incomplete; director cuts at "Are you kidding me?": actor added word "precious" to end of line.

TAKE 2: Same. Incomplete. Actor giggled.

TAKE 3: Same. Incomplete. After "ass," actress rushes at director, beats severely. Remainder of day spent testing FX.

In Bel Air, in a beamed and darkened study, wan firelight flickered on wormwood walls and on mounted stuffed game heads and bug-eyed fish so many in number they fairly teemed. Zelig, in a red and gold silken bathrobe and reeking of his favorite splash-on essence, an exotic cologne called Definition of Gross, was trilling in a loveseat close by the fire, excitedly awaiting the evening's promise. Sprightly was coming. She had called. It was a deal. Smiling at a dying fire's red-glowing embers, listening to the cracklings of a burnt-out log, he adjusted his mask—he'd selected the Phantom for this night—and savored psychiatric miracles to come. The champagne was on ice; perhaps tonight he would be able to check the label.

Anxious, he'd begun to softly sing, "C'mon 'a My House" when abruptly he hushed and cocked an ear. Footsteps! His heart began to lope. It was she! The brittle steps on an outside pebbled path crunched steadily closer to the study's open doors that led out to the patio, garden and grounds.

"I've been waiting for you, darling," rasped the mogul.

"Yeah yeah yeah."

She was standing in the doorway leading in from the garden, dressed, in accordance with Zelig's instructions, in only her mink,

stiletto-heeled shoes, a pearl necklace and a bracelet around her ankle so that he could tell her left leg from her right.

"Don't sing," she gritted. "Don't sing one note or I'm gone."

She glanced around with distaste at the animals and fish shot and hooked by other people whom Zelig paid to do it. He had also hired people to ski for him in Aspen. He held out his arms to her.

"Come to me, sweetheart."

"Not yet. You got the paper?"

"Must we really talk business now, heartbeat?"

"We must."

He sighed. "Very well, then; have it your way."

He slipped a typed document out of his pocket and rustled it loudly as he held it aloft.

"As you asked."

"Is it notarized?" she said.

"Yes. And witnessed."

For the total consideration of one U.S. dollar, the blue-bound, three-page document promised, Jason Hazard was guaranteed his three-picture deal irrespective of performance as director on *The Satanist*.

"Here it is," the mogul teased her, waving it. "Come."

Sprightly walked slowly, her heels clicking loudly on the old pine planks of the study floor. She stopped about a foot out of Zelig's reach, leaned over and snatched the papers out of his hand.

Zelig groped in the air for her leg.

"Love, come closer," he hissed.

"Bull-*shit*! You're not laying a hand on me until I've read this!"

"Of course."

"Yeah, you bet, *of course*."

"Go right ahead. Though I must admit to a certain disappointment. I expected some tenderness."

"Is that in this paper?"

"I forgot it."

"Too bad. Go fire your lawyers."

Frowning, Sprightly moved the papers closer to the fire. "I can't read this," she complained, leaning over, "it's too dark. Put on some lights so I can see the fucking fine print, Arthur."

"No, no lights. They're so formal; so cold; so unromantic. Here, I'll throw another log on the fire," he said suavely.

He leaned over and groped with his hands, and, mistaking a stuffed blue marlin for a log, he detached it from the wall and smoothly tossed it at the fireplace. It missed the firepit opening completely and shattered a decorative mirror on the hearth.

He sat motionless. "Clumsy," he quietly uttered.

"Jesus!"

Sprightly dropped the papers, turned around, shook her head and strode deliberately away towards the garden door.

"I can't do it," she murmured. "I just can't fucking do it."

Seconds later Zelig's butler stiffed into the room.

"Can I help you, sir?"

"Scythrop, what broke?"

"It would appear to be a fireplace mirror."

"Seven years bad luck," the mogul said tonelessly.

"Shall I rescue the marlin?"

"What marlin?"

"The one in the fireplace, sir."

"Not our problem."

Hazard was late getting home; he'd been working with his editor, "Total" Transformation, on assemblies of scenes that had been shot and were complete. He was carrying a large thin pepperoni pizza and was wearing his usual demented grin. "Hey, anybody home, guys? Joey's was closed but I picked up a pizza. Come and get it while it's hot."

It was after eleven.

"Sprightly? Ralph?"

There was no response. Hazard kicked the front door shut behind him, set down the pizza on the entry hall hutch and moved into the living room. The lights were all on, including those that bathed the ocean. He stared. The door to the deck was open. He moved to it and looked outside. The deck was empty. Where were Sprightly and Ralph?

Forty minutes later, the director was sunk in an overstuffed chair beside the living room fireplace. Rain had come spattering down on the roof, and he'd started a roaring pine log fire, manically devoured the entire pizza, then downed a double scotch, collapsed into the chair, put his feet up on a hassock and his mind on hold. After a time he fell into a sleep. It would prove to hold the answer to all of his cares.

Part Seven

DELIVERANCE

"*Friend,*" *said the Spirit.* "*Could you, only for a moment, fix your mind on something not yourself?*"

—C. S. LEWIS,
The Great Divorce

CHAPTER ONE

"HAZARD, SAHIB!"

Hazard groggily opened an eye. The fire had dwindled to glowing little memories and Ralph was bending over him, shaking his arm.

"Hunh?"

"Evil doings, sahib! Bad! Coming quickly!"

Hazard roused himself fully and stood up.

"What's the matter?"

Ralph beckoned with a finger.

"Come with guru!"

Hazard followed Ralph up the staircase. As they came to the landing and approached the master bedroom, a voice from within abruptly burst into song:

"The hills are alive with the sound of music . . ."

Hazard froze in his tracks. He was hearing the voice of Julie Andrews. He lowered his face into a hand. "Ah, my God!" Julie Andrews and her husband, Blake Edwards, lived nearby.

"Sahib hear it?"

The director looked up, at first relieved, but then he met Ralph's gaze and became uneasy. The Hindu's huge saffron-coated eyes were wide and he was rolling them around like Harpo Marx. *Something's terribly wrong with this picture,* thought Hazard. *Ralph is never this broad; he underplays.* He glanced around; everything was strange: an odd dimness, the proportion of things, an almost visible thickening of the air. It might have been a scene that had been shot by Smoke Barbie.

Suddenly a blast of icy air hit the landing and the song was at earsplitting volume for a moment as the door rattled open and Sprightly rushed out.

"My heart wants to sing every song it—"

She slammed the door shut behind her. Her eyes were two blank Little Orphan Annie ovals of incredulity and shock. "Holy shit, am I glad to get out of there," she shivered. "God, that room is like *ice!*"

Hazard moved to her swiftly.

"What's happening?"

"Barbra's possessed!"

He cuffed her on the cheek. "Come out of it!"

He paused to flick a deadpan glance at the door as the singing abruptly cut off in mid-phrase. *"Of all the gin joints in the world, she walks into mine,"* growled the voice of Humphrey Bogart in *Casablanca.*

Hazard's gaze drooped forebodingly to Sprightly.

"That was Barbra!" she huskily intoned.

Hazard made to move past her. "The TV must be on."

"No, sahib! Do not go! Very bad!" warned Ralph.

The guru had leaped to block the door.

"This is *movie* demon, sahib! Very dangerous!"

"Ralph thinks that they're after you," warned Sprightly. "I mean, demonwise."

Ralph put a finger to his lips, hissing, "Listen!"

"That's what they call a sanity clause."

"You can't fool me: there ain't *no sanity clause . . ."*

Hazard's eyes glazed over.

"It's a Marx Brothers movie," he intoned.

Then with sudden resolve he pushed past Ralph, pulled open the door and entered the room. Except for the nightlights' glow, it was dark. Unaware of the door clicking shut behind him, Hazard shivered, amazed that his breath was coming frosty, and he peered around the room with narrowed eyes, half-expecting to discover Franz Detritus and his crew. When his gaze fell on Barbra he froze in shock: the cat, sitting up in the middle of the bed, had expanded to triple its normal size, and was staring malevolently at

Hazard with spiteful yellow eyes that shot through him like a curse.

"Barbra?" quavered Hazard.

The cat's mouth moved up and down as if in speech.

"I'm not Barbra," came a guttural, impossibly deep voice.

Hazard's hair stood on end.

"Could ya help an old altar cat, Father?"

Hazard bolted from the room and slammed the door shut. From behind it came music that sounded like the clopping of hooves, and the voice of a western singer:

"The noonday train will bring Frank Miller . . ."

Sprightly turned a wasted look to her husband.

"Shane?" she asked hopelessly.

"High Noon."

Deep into the witchcraft of that night, the Hazards and Ralph were at the dining room table. Sprightly had taken up smoking again and had mounded crumpled butts in a seashell ashtray, while Ralph pored over innumerable books that were opened to underlined passages and pages. Hazard, his forehead shaded by a hand, thought bleakly of Jonathan Drood and Elvis and then flicked his gaze up at the dining room ceiling and the muffled sounds of a quiet dialogue scene in the original *Godfather* movie:

"Someday I may come to you for a favor."

"Every sentence ever spoken," Hazard uttered in a monotone, "is still floating around up in space." He lowered his unreadable gaze to Sprightly. "Maybe these just finally landed on this house."

"Sure, Jason—you have rational answers for everything."

The bite in her voice was not entirely distanced from Hazard's first thought in the search for solutions; namely, to telephone the Agoura Animal Shelter and report the Himalayan as a stray. "Let them come and pick her up," the director had reasoned; "no one has to mention that we think she's possessed."

"Hazard, sahib!"

Hazard's hooded gaze shifted to the guru.

"Something now very clear to me, sahib."

"Yes?"

"You are definitely principal target of this demon."

"How so?"

"Please to notice every word demon saying is coming from movie that has gone into profit."

"Hindu asshole."

"Demon taunting you, sahib."

"Demon taunting me?"

Ralph's chutney-stained index finger tapped at a passage in a book he was holding. "Yes, everything totally clear," he said, nodding. "I read now from famous holy paperback book."

The lights in the room began rapidly flickering, dimmed to an amber murk and then died. Even the nightlights were completely extinguished.

"Go ahead, Ralph."

"Cannot read in dark, sahib."

"I understand."

Abruptly the room began to quiver, and soon it was violently pitching and shaking, sending cloudlets of plaster crickling down from the ceiling; then, as suddenly, everything settled and was quiet.

"Could you give us just the broad strokes, Ralph?"

"We must bringing in priest."

"You mean an *exorcism?*"

Ralph nodded.

"Are you crazy? They'll start calling us a problem picture! We can't bring outsiders into this!" declared Hazard.

"Well, we've got to do *something*," Sprightly insisted.

"Just a minute, I've got an idea," Hazard blurted. He stood up and looked off with a visionary gleam, the crooked grin and mad stare back in glorious bloom. "I'll do it myself!" he declared.

"Do what?" Sprightly asked.

"The exorcism!" he crowed.

Upstairs Tom and Jerry began a chase.

The next thing that the director was clearly aware of, in the first of a puzzling series of fugues, was of driving to Our Lady of Malibu Church, breaking in and, with furtive, crafty eyes, siphoning holy water from a font in the back of the church with a kitchen bulb baster, then returning to the house where he displayed it victoriously and squeezed the holy water into a vial.

"You can't do this!" Sprightly said to him, fearful and taut as he stood outside the door to the bedroom holding a copy of the *Roman Ritual* open to the prayers of the Rite for Exorcism.

"Why not?" Hazard asked her blandly.

"You aren't a priest!" she said.

"How the fuck would the *cat* know that?"

He held up the holy water vial with a leer: "Don't worry—I've got dynamite here in a bottle!"

Hazard turned to the door with a look of surmise as conversation from *The Philadelphia Story* broke off. He heard deep low chuckling, then that guttural, malevolent voice as it liltingly invited him, "Come in!"

Hazard opened the door and as he entered the bedroom a bolt of freezing air hit his face. He squinted. Behind him the door slammed shut and when his eyes had opened fully he stepped backward and goggled: Barbra, now grown to enormous size, was on her back and was strapped by her paws and feet to the rugged wooden posts of the bed, which, quite unaccountably, were now padded. Once again Hazard felt that odd sense of the surreal.

"You remember that night in the Garden?"

The nasal, thin voice was coming out of the cat.

"You came down to my dressing room and said, 'Kid, this ain't

your night; we're going for the price on Wilson.' You remember that?"

Brando in *On the Waterfront!*

Hazard's jaw clenched tight—another hit!

"Just shut up with that stuff," he said coldly. "You don't know what you're dealing with here, you dumb cat."

"You was my brother, Charley. You shoulda looked out for me a little."

"That does it!"

Hazard angrily lifted the holy water vial and snapped off a sprinkle at the cat. Barbra's face contorted hideously, and she writhed and yowled in pain, making sounds that only Pavarotti's wife had ever heard. Then abruptly the bone-chilling cries broke off as the cat stared at Hazard with hateful malevolence:

"You're dead on this waterfront, and every waterfront from Boston to New Orleans!" snarled Lee J. Cobb in the role of Johnny Friendly. *"You don't drive a truck or a cab! You don't push a baggage rack! You don't work no place! You're dead!"*

The room began to rumble and tilt and great fissures in the plaster walls cracked open. Mesmerized, Hazard backed slowly toward the door as the voice of Lee Cobb changed to that of John Wayne:

"I'll catch up with you. I don't know when but I'll catch up. And every time you turn around, expect to see me because one time you'll turn around and I'll be there. I'll kill you, Matt."

Another giant hit—*Red River!*

"You evil fuck!" seethed Hazard.

He heard an odd sound of compressed air escaping. He gaped. Like a float in the Macy's parade at the end of the day when the helium hissed out, the bloated demonic cat was shrinking.

"What a world, what a world!" grieved the wicked witch in *The Wizard of Oz.*

The director cursed beneath his breath.

When Barbra had subsided to her normal size, Hazard warily returned to the foot of the bed, whereon the cat looked up with drowsy, wet eyes, and then put down her head and appeared to nap. The director looked over his shoulder at the door and called out jubilantly, "It worked! Now I'll say a few prayers to cinch the deal!" But when he turned back the cat was leering at him. "*The race goes on, Judah*," it gasped in the voice of Messala in *Ben Hur*. Hazard's grin turned to porcelain, slowly discolored, then shattered and tinkled to the floor in blue bits.

"*It goes on!*"

"Hey, Jason!"

A sleepy-eyed figure was tapping at the glass of the beach-side door. It was Tony DeSky. Hazard rushed to unlock the door and let him in.

"Thanks for coming, Tony. Sorry I had to wake you."

"Hey, don't mention it," the barefooted agent drawled in his boozy, sandpaper-textured voice. Wearing flannel pajama tops, bush jacket and khaki trousers with the bottoms rolled up, he gripped a brown leather briefcase trimmed in brass and with the hand that was holding a lit cigar he made vague little circling gestures toward his feet. "You don't mind a little sand on your floor?"

"It's not a problem."

The agent took a meeting with the Hazards and Ralph in the course of which his calm, bemused expression never changed, and in the end he decided he would look for himself. He went up to the bedroom and entered it alone, and in less than half a minute emerged pale and shaken. "Yeah, you got yourselves a problem here, guys," he said, nodding. "Whaddya say we have a beer and take another little meeting? Okay? Let's kick this crazy thing around a few minutes."

At the dining room table, the agent summed it up:

"Look, you tried, you couldn't handle it yourself, we need a priest. So you want an insider? Great. We got one. Vogel is already on the payroll, right? So if we use him you save a few bucks on the budget. Besides, he's supposed to be pretty hot shit on this stuff. I mean, why are we kockin' around? In the meantime, I'll book you a coupla backups, some real heavy hitters that I think could do the gig." While he spoke, he'd unbuckled the leather briefcase, and from it he fished a few eight-by-ten glossies, various head shots of smiling priests. With his cigar hand, he tapped at the photo on top. "Now this guy here is pure dynamite," he told them. "I've seen him work. A great talent."

Hazard peered at the photo, looking puzzled. "This man . . ."

"Father Lucius Venom," drawled DeSky.

"I could swear it's Don Rickles," the director marveled in a reference to the stand-up insult comedian.

"None of our business," DeSky said mysteriously. He slipped the photograph back into the briefcase. "In the meantime, now, what about this *Roman Ritual* thing? We gotta sew up the rights to that too."

"You mean the rights to the Catholic ritual of exorcism?" the director inquired dubiously.

"Yeah, that's right," said DeSky with a nod. His hands made a globe-shaping gesture. "It's a package."

There began a swift series of attempts at exorcism, beginning at two in the morning when a Yellow Cab pulled up to the house and disgorged Father Vogel and a snarling pit bull.

"Okay, Lance," Vogel quietly urged him. "Here we go!"

In the foyer the Jesuit met Hazard and Sprightly. DeSky had the priest sign a standard release plus an agency representation agreement, then ventured to the kitchen for another beer. From upstairs a scene from *Gone with the Wind* drifted down.

"I don't know nothin' about birthin' no babies, Miss Scarlett!"

Vogel glared up toward the master bedroom with a silent snarl of contempt and hate.

"That's her," Sprightly told him. "That's Barbra."

The priest looked down at her incredulously, a faint anger twisting his lips. "You said *her*? Lady, that was your *first* mistake: that's not your cat up there!" he said coldly.

"Don't you want to hear the background of the case?" Hazard asked him.

"Listen, stow it! I know what I'm doing, okay? Good old Lance'll tear the ears and ass off that demon!"

Sprightly paled. "My poor Barbra?"

Vogel's eyebrows bushed together.

"Look, lady, you keep making that same mistake. Now you listen: that thing up there in your bedroom is not your Barbra. You got that, airhead? It's all Dominations and Thrones and Powers and unseen forces out the kazoo. I've done a million of these things, they're all alike. Now step aside. We'll clean this up for you guys in two seconds."

When Vogel and the dog went up into the bedroom, the dialogue from *Gone with the Wind* sharply ended and an ominous stillness pressed down upon the house. On the landing, the Hazards could hear the dog snarl and Father Vogel's voice quavering, "Now listen to me, asshole!" Seconds later the door burst open, however, and the pit bull scampered out yelping and yipping, raced across the landing and down the stairs. Vogel emerged looking drawn and shut the door. He found a cigarette, lit it, took a drag, exhaled it. "Look, I think you've got a problem," he tremulously uttered. "This thing's not exactly what your agent told me. I'm out of it. Okay? It's just not my bag."

He headed for the stairs. "Hey, Lance! Wait up!"

Hazard opened the bedroom door and peered in. On the bed in place of Barbra was a fiendishly grinning, three-hundred-pound rat with gleaming foot-long, razor-sharp fangs.

"I told him to get a life," it drooled. "Who's next?"

The answer was a squat and balding priest with a truculent grin and mocking eyes that shone with a subtly demonic hostility. Hazard appraised him with a look of confusion.

"Excuse me, but aren't you Don Rickles?" he asked him.

"I am Father Lucius Venom. You called?"

"Vennommmmmmm!" roared a fiendish voice from above.

GET A LIFE!

The next second the house gave a jolting shudder.

Venom glanced up toward the bedroom sardonically.

"Oh, and have we got a naughty kitty in the house?"

The priest chuckled, then he trotted upstairs, removed his coat and went into the bedroom with his head tilted forward like an eager and bloodthirsty matador. The enormous rat had disappeared, supplanted by the giant, tied-down cat. "You're going to die in here, Venom!" the demonic feline boomed in that guttural, deep male voice.

In that moment the bed levitated four feet.

Venom's mocking eyes and grin remained fixed.

"Cute—have you tried this act in Vegas? At the Grand they make Siberian tigers disappear. We could work you in tomorrow with a Viennese juggling act that makes strudel while they balance on a wire and tell pointless jokes in German. Whoopee-doo!"

Venom reached out and tugged down on a bedpost and instantly the bed crashed down to the floor.

Venom chuckled.

"Cute whiskers. Did you grow them yourself, or did you steal them from Don Corleone's old pasta?"

The room began violently tilting and shaking. Windows shattered. The demonic cat arched and snarled and spat.

Venom lowered his head and chuckled.

"Gee, the room is shaking. Isn't that impressive? I'm scared, I'm just pissing in my pants from total terror." He reached into his cassock to a trouser pocket, withdrew a large biscuit and tossed it to the cat. "Here's a cookie, kid. Suck on the raisins for a while and pretend that you're Frank singing 'Nancy' in Fresno."

"You know, a funny thing happened to me coming here tonight."

The corners of Venom's mouth turned down. The cat had been replaced by the comic, Rodney Dangerfield, who began to spew a stream of one-liners. Livid, Venom turned on his heel and left the room. On the landing, while picking up his coat and departing, he said harshly and tersely: "I work alone."

Here Hazard was suddenly conscious again of the strange, surreal quality of everything around him, of a blurry kaleidoscoping of events. He was aware of two exorcists arriving in a long black van with blackout windows and fluorescent white crosses on its sides and on the hood. They insisted on a fifty-dollar payment in advance. "No, that's for the both of us, lady," said the one with the long, livid scar on his face and the heavy New York gangster accent. He had introduced himself with a business card as Father Joseph "Joey" Spinnel, "The Singing Exorcist" from Rome. His accompanist, a short and husky priest introduced as Father Salvatore Giancana, but who powerfully resembled the actor Burt Young, gripped the handle of a rather large violin case and exuded a particularly menacing aura, especially when everyone at last understood that he would play his accompaniment on a piano.

"Yeah, we'd like it in cash," Luciano told Sprightly.

Abruptly he sneezed. He hauled out a handkerchief and glanced around the room.

"You got cats in the house?" he asked. "I'm allergic."

It was here that Hazard's world began to spin and grow wavery, and then everything in it disappeared and the director was standing near the foot of the bed where in a twinkling the demonic cat evanesced and was supplanted by a scowling human figure in an army coat and a World War I Prussian helmet.

Hazard gasped.

"Ja, it's me," nodded Jesús Machtmeintag, "not a rotten undigested bit of bratwurst. Notice I am here against my wishes," he grumped. "Why should I help you? I hate you. Never mind. Zey have sent me because we are zer same: we are too much obsessive-compulsive monomaniacs. We are also big shitheads besides."

"Someone sent you?"

"Zey."

"Who is *zey?*"

"Floyd Gott."

Hazard looked down and shook his head. "This isn't real," he decided. "I'm dreaming."

"*Ja, ja,* you are dreaming, ziss iss altogezzer true, but also it is real as well, Jew director. Ziss is not now Geraldo mit poltergeist horsecrap, *leben-nach-leben* baloney in zer tunnel. Ziss iss big-time supernatural phenomena, *dummkopf.* Pay attention! Floyd Gott he is sending three spirits. I am zer first und zer most important, zer Spirit of July Fourth Opening Veekend. Ziss is zer biggest B.O. zair can be. I have to find out from you right now ziss moment you are going to be willing uzzer spirits should come."

"What other spirits?"

"Of Labor Day Veekend Past und zer Spirit of Easter Release to Come."

"How come you're helping me?" asked the director.

"For two hours every week zey have promised I don't splice."

"Where are you?" asked Hazard, abruptly suspicious.

"Never mind. But I give you ziss vun little clue: everyone is vaiting for Franz Detritus."

Suddenly Machtmeintag disappeared and another, slimmer figure took his place in the bed. A wooden chair slid rapidly across the room and hit Hazard with a thump in the back of the legs.

"Here's looking at you, kid," growled Humphrey Bogart.

He lay atop the covers in his Sam Spade trenchcoat smoking a Lucky Strike cigarette. "Come on and have a seat, kid, okay? Just relax. I think it's time for us talk a little common sense."

Goggle-eyed and star-struck, Hazard sat down.

"You oughta open some windows in here, it's kinda stuffy," said the Bogart apparition with a tic and a grimace. Instantly, a window flew up with a bang and cool sea air wafted into the room. "Nice breeze. It's always cool near the waters," said the specter. "I like these little holidays away from the heat."

"Where have you come from?" asked Hazard with a frown of apprehension.

"We're all waiting for Detritus," said the spirit enigmatically. He took the cigarette from his lips and cupped his hand underneath it to catch a long ash. He glanced around. "You got an ashtray anyplace, pal? I keep tryin' to quit but it's tough, it's tough." His mouth twitched upward at the corners in a tic as he scanned the debris in the room from all the shaking. He picked up a broken piece of vase from a bedstand. "Never mind, kid, I'll use this," he said. Scowling, he carefully chipped off the ash and then earnestly peered back up at Hazard. "Can we talk? I mean really lay it out on the line? 'Kay." He reached a hand into a pocket of his coat and extracted a pair of steel ball bearings. He commenced to lightly click them around in his hand. "It's about your movies," he softly growled. "I'll have to admit that I've only seen three of them; they've been easy on me lately, I've been good. But let me tell you . . ." He briefly held his nose. "Stinkeroo."

Hazard glared.

Bogart shrugged. "Honest criticism, kiddo."

"Are you sure you're not the Devil?" the director asked tartly.

"I'm not sayin' that I am, I'm not sayin' that I'm not."

Hazard stared at the figure in the bed with sudden fear interlarded with surliness and sulk, and for a time there was silence. Then Hazard cleared his throat.

"Which three did you see?" he inquired weakly.

" 'Kay. I've seen *Illegible, Autumn*—"

"You didn't like *Illegible?*" yipped Hazard.

Bogart grimaced.

"There wasn't any love in it, kiddo; no caring, same as both those other turkeys that I saw. They didn't light any candles or tickle any ribs, they didn't feed any hungry kids or souls. All I saw in those films was you playing with your putz. I've got to wonder how your wife is ever going to get pregnant."

"I don't know what you're talking about," said Hazard.

"All of your sex drive goes into your movies."

Bogart tamped out the cigarette butt and scowled.

"Look, I think it's really time we got down to the short strokes," he growled. "My business with you is the past; that's my assignment. I'm going to show you what happens when a guy runs around inside the squirrel cage of his ego."

The corners of his mouth twitched up convulsively.

"Get ready—*you're taking the fall!*"

Immediately, Hazard had a near-death experience: in a single, panoramic flash he reviewed every frame of every film he'd ever made in what seemed to endure for no more than an instant, though in certain respects it was more like eons:

Every character was played by Hazard.

"Hiya, roomie!" said a voice. "You fock my seester?"

Hazard startled. Then he rubbed at his eyes and looked again.

"Floyd!" he yelled joyously.

"Yeah, it's me."

Floyd God was on the bed in place of Bogart and was wearing a silvery, metallic jumpsuit like Raymond Massey's in *War of the Worlds*. "I just thought I ought to come here and do this myself," he said in that leaf-rustling, breathy mumble.

"I'm so damn glad to see you!" said Hazard. He meant it. He felt like embracing his old friend warmly, but was wary of electromagnetic unknowns. "Even though I'm only dreaming this," he added. "*Am* I dreaming?"

"It's a dream, but it's real," said Floyd.

Hazard nodded. "Yeah, somebody said that. Anyway, how are you? What happened to you, Floyd?"

God answered but Hazard merely stared at him blankly.

"Floyd, you've got to speak up. I just can't understand you."

"Yeah, okay."

"How'd you die, Floyd?"

"Die? Who's dead? I've been on another planet, the planet Nookie. They allowed me to teleport down for a while."

Now Hazard took note of a small round insignia high on the chest of the silvery suit, a single, well-shaped female breast intertwined with an elegant letter "N." It appeared to be made of some shining metal.

Floyd glanced at his watch. "I can't stay here too long, old roomie. I've got to get back to my wife and kid."

"You're married? A kid? *You?*"

"Yeah, me. I've got to tell you, Jason, that's where it's at. It's the answer. All those years I didn't want to quit being a kid, of just wanting to keep playing with the blocks and toys. Yeah, I guess it was compulsive with me. You, too, though. With you, instead of babes, it's your work, your movies. It's all the same thing: it's all about the size of your dick. It's dumb. Have a kid. You'll start to think of someone else.

"Anyway, these Nookians," Floyd continued, "they came down and abducted me. They had this crisis. They were all dying out. No potent men. They got into some kind of a war and got zapped by some vicious planetwide radiation; those fucking Ferengis, maybe, or the Klingons—somehow they'd learned to split the atom of a fart. So the Nookians needed me pretty badly, and, hell, I was happy to help all I could. But you know, I got tired of it, Jason. I did. I mean, how many women do you have to screw before you're convinced you're an okay guy? How many good movies do you have to make? Anyway, maybe because it was forbidden, all I finally wanted was just one woman. They said, fine, fulfill your quota for one more year and we'll allow you to live out your perverted fantasy. Ah, well, hell—do you know what it's like to be *forced* to screw a whole bunch of different women? Well, I did it and I got to pick just one girl. And I'm happy. I'm not restless. I'm finally really happy. It all fell together when Nearly came along."

"Nearly?"

"My son. I just love him to pieces. I find I'm always wanting to do something for him. That's what's opened the door for me to loving other people: having someone else to live for, someone else's happiness to always be thinking about. I can't describe it; I can't even explain it. All I know is doing something for somebody else is the only thing that really can make someone happy. Yeah, I know this is all dead news, it's been around; but we get fucked up because we really don't *believe* it. It just doesn't seem possible. It didn't to me. You don't know until you actually go and do it."

Hazard hear a sound like a distant engine or bees in a meadow long ago. Floyd glanced out a window. "I haven't much time," he said, "and I owe you for all of your dates that I screwed. That's why I volunteered for this, this is payback. So listen, I've arranged for a little surprise. I'm going to show you the future, Jason. You're going to see your new movie all edited and mixed and scored, completely finished. Pay particular attention to the musical number where you browbeat my sister into showing her tits."

"Where I *what?*"

"You'll see."

"I would *never* use Sprightly like that! That's outrageous!" bridled the director.

"Never mind, just pay attention to the movie. And just one more thing," said Floyd, looking grave. "It's important."

"What's that?"

"Please fuck my sister."

Hazard would remember nothing more of Floyd, for suddenly all he could see and hear was a widescreen running of a finished *The Satanist* from the first fade-in to fade-out. Though it took but an instant, he saw it with a cold and brutal clarity, which is to say, through the eyes of someone sane; and as he watched, he gripped the sides of his face in horror.

"My God!" he cried out. "My God! What have I done?"

"Jason?"

Someone was shaking him. Sprightly.

"Jason, wake up! Come on! Wake up!"

He opened his eyes and had to shake off an impulse to throw open a window and find some child who would run to the market and buy him a goose, for he felt an enormous sense of relief. He squinted at Sprightly bending over him. She was wearing her long mink coat.

"You were having some nightmare," she said with a frown.

For a moment he stared in disorientation; then the *Satanist* film of his dream flashed back to him in a wave of engulfing despair.

Sprightly's look of concern began to deepen.

"Whenever you sleep you scream out loud," she lamented. "You didn't used to do that, Jason."

His brow furrowed up and he stared at her earnestly.

"Sprightly—what did you think of *Illegible?*"

"What kind of a question is that?"

"I don't know."

He folded his arms, hunched over and shivered.

"Jesus, it's cold in here," he murmured.

Sprightly said, "Throw another fish on the fire."

He looked up at her. "What?"

She shook her head. "Never mind." She spread apart her mink, disclosing her nakedness. "You wanna fuck?" she asked him bluntly.

Hazard stared fixedly at her charms. He was thinking of the strange vivid dream and of Floyd.

"Yes."

"I'm in shock," said Sprightly. "I'm floored."

He nodded mutely and thoughtfully, continuing to stare.

Maybe it would work, he was thinking; *yeah, maybe. I mean, shit—those are really fantastic tits!*

CHAPTER TWO

THE TWENTY-FOOT-LONG white Mercedes limousine with the black-out windows and FLAUNT IT license plates crept moodily in Friday night traffic en route to the pagodas and movie star foot-steps-in-cement of the Hollywood Chinese Theater and the long-awaited world premiere of *The Satanist*. Inside, on mink-lined upholstery, rode two men in Armani tuxedos and a traveling tank that contained a snake.

"Did they change my script very much, Mr. Zelig?" asked the childlike, trusting voice of Drood.

"Ah, well, only the musical sequence, Jonathan."

"Musical sequence?"

"Don't worry. You'll like it."

Drood lowered his head, seemed to listen, and then nodded.

"Yes," he said finally. "I think that I will."

He looked up at the mogul, who sat opposite him.

"I'm so sorry that you're blind, Mr. Zelig."

"That's kind of you. Most people are."

At the confluence of Hollywood and Vine, the mogul turned his head to gaze idly out a window at the weekly public scourging of studio executives caught reading manuscripts, screenplays or treatments prior to announcing their acquisition, as opposed to relying on the usual reports from their volunteer staffs of twelve-year-old readers.

"I really like your face, Mr. Zelig."

The mogul turned and stared for a moment.

"My mask, you mean, Jonathan?"

"Oh. It's a mask?"

"Yes. It's a mask. It's Charo. Tell me, how are they treating you, Jonathan?"

"Oh, fine."

"I'm so glad they let you out for this tonight."

"I wouldn't miss it for the world, Mr. Zelig."

"Yes, Jonathan; and neither, quite frankly, would I."

Five months had passed since Sprightly had spurned him. The hope of his sick imagination relied upon this evening's humiliation of Hazard and its aftermath of media outrage and scorn; somehow, he pondered, as he stared distractedly at the mugging of an elderly tourist by a man in an ape suit with a yellow revolver concealed amid a cluster of ripe bananas, Sprightly might yet become disillusioned. But if not, he was still guaranteed his revenge, for the evening's boos for Hazard, and its hisses—here the mogul's quick gaze shifted over to Jeff and the festive pink ribbons tied and bowed around his neck—were a tonic that his heart foresaw with eagerness, if not with unbridled joy. *As for me, who will blame me?* the mogul reflected; *everybody knows that I'm totally crazy, maybe even the craziest man on earth!*

"Simpson thinks your snake is a very nice person."

The mogul turned his mask to the author inscrutably.

"Is that so?" he said after a moment.

"He wants to know where he can send him some poems that he's written. They're pretty. They're all about rice."

Maybe not the craziest, Zelig amended.

The mogul returned his gaze to the window. They were a block from the entrance to the theater and already he could hear the fans cheering the stars as they arrived in tuxedos and formal gowns. Zelig had insisted on a "world premiere" complete with all its trappings and hullabaloo—the invited celebrities and television interviews, the spotlights and a swarming press—in order to maximize Hazard's disgrace. In addition, all the West Coast reviewers would be there. As for the national critical establishment, Zelig had arranged a simultaneous screening at New York's 69th Regiment Armory with mats on the floor for seating. The printed and beguiling four-color invitation specified "gala reception beforehand featuring popcorn, Milk Duds and Coke," and beneath it, the allurement in large block letters: "ALL YOU CAN EAT! FREE! FREE!"

"Are you ready for your interview, Jonathan?"

"Yes."

Zelig turned to him.

"You sound a little blue. Are you blue?"

"I hate it when they call me the Prince of Darkness, Mr. Zelig."

"Yes, I hate it when they call me that, too."

Drood made an odd little groaning sound, then he sighed and turned his head to stare glumly out the window. "My wife came to visit last week. She says she wants to try and get back together."

"Does that please you?"

"I don't know, Mr. Zelig. All those cats. Electricity makes you see a bunch of things differently."

"Jonathan?"

The author turned his gaze to the mogul.

"Yes, sir?"

"You remember about your interview, Jonathan?"

"Interview?"

"In front of the theater. With the man. You remember? You remember what it is you're going to say?"

"How Mr. Hazard told Simpson what to tell me to write?"

"Do we need to drag Simpson into this, Jonathan? Perhaps the chain of authorship should be more direct."

"I'm scared the Writer's Guild might hurt me if I do that, Mr. Zelig."

"I'll take care of that."

"Okay, I'll remember, Mr. Zelig."

The author turned his moody gaze back to the window and gloomed, "I just don't want any credit arbitrations."

Far behind them, a dusty, blue Lincoln sedan tooled along with Tony DeSky at the wheel and, beside him, slumped down in the passenger's seat, a miserable, catatonic Hazard in a tux. DeSky tapped lightly on his car horn and waved at a large group of men in an open truck that had just pulled in ahead of them. The band of broadly smiling Mexicans waved back. "Patsy invited them," he said without expression. "Everybody's comin' tonight except Sprightly. Too bad. I really think she shoulda come," the agent rued. Drawn by the flashing red light of a squad car, he glanced to the right where he glimpsed a policeman slipping the cuffs on an out-of-work studio head who had burst into Musso-Frank's and demanded the liver and onions at gunpoint.

"Yeah," he said, nodding his head; "She shoulda come."

Earlier that day in the Malibu Colony, the Hazards had debated the wisdom of attending. Hazard, with a sentence of death at his throat, had paced with a Cajun martini in his hand while Sprightly sat knitting in a chair at the bar. She was wearing a housecoat and fluffy slippers.

"I'm not going," she repeated, her eyes on her work.

"But you've *got* to."

"No, I don't," she said tautly. "*You've* got to. You let him put it into that stupid damned contract."

"You're the star. If you're not there, it's going to look pretty strange."

"I'm just not gonna sit there while they look at my tits!"

Hazard stopped pacing, silenced. He walked behind the bar and took a breath. "You want a drink?"

She shook her head and said, "No. I'm not drinking."

"Yeah, that's right," he said, scrounging in a bucket for some ice. "You haven't been drinking at all these days. How come?"

She shrugged. "I dunno. Not in the mood."

He sipped at his drink. "What's that you're knitting?"

"I don't know yet," she answered.

"In development?"

Despite herself she nodded and smiled good-naturedly as she expertly flipped another thread. "Yeah, Jason. In development. Right. That's right." She looked up. "You all packed?"

They were booked on American at noon the next day. Hazard planned to lie low in their Connecticut hideaway for six months while he polished a script, his magnum opus, designed to be shot on location in Egypt.

He said, "Yeah, I'm all packed; packed and ready to go." He knocked back the dregs of his spicy martini and quickly went to work at building another. Sprightly darted looks of concern.

"You gonna have any more of those?" she asked.

He said, "Ten."

They heard a door close. Ralph had padded in off the beach. "Very much of good luck tonight, sahib. Everyone in whole Colony talking."

Hazard felt a headache coming on. "Thanks, Ralph."

The guru clasped his hands together, bowed deep and then flapped to the kitchen on sandy bare feet. Hazard watched him flowing away like the Ganges, brown and muddy and unweeting of his care. "So, okay, I'll go with Tony tonight," he said morosely.

He took his martini with him up the bedroom; time to shave and get dressed for his public execution. Once in the room, though, he felt a depression and he miserably sank to the edge of the bed, where he hung his head and fozzed his fate. Since the night that Charles Dickens and Andy Warhol had united to bizarrely invade his dreams, the director had fitfully wrestled with integrity; his manic mien had vanished, and he looked at the project just as it was and untinted by ludicrous rationalizations. He had even accepted his failures of the past. But like a rabid and maddened Nosferatu, he'd been unable to pull his frenzied fangs from the throat of the Zelig three-picture deal. *This really isn't me*, he now argued again to himself; *it has nothing to do with my work: every frame of this movie is Arthur Zelig's from the first fade-in to the last fade-out. I have nothing whatever to be ashamed of*, he went on to delude himself again: *I've learned a lot. My next film will be my finest. They'll forget this. I know what I'm doing. It's all right.* Suddenly Hazard came crashing to earth as a line from the musical sequence assailed him, the striking refrain, *"Get out of that cat!"* He lowered his head with a quiet groan. *It will soon be all over,* he tried to assure himself; *it will be over and buried and gone.* He looked up through a window at far Catalina and thought once again of his extraordinary dream. *Yeah, alright, so I'm selfish and completely self-centered and a user and abuser of Sprightly and a prick. So what do you want from me? I'm an artist!*

He'd recounted the dream to Isadore Shriek, placing stress on its quality of total reality. "Did you like that?" Shriek had interrupted him; "I can give you that high anytime," and, so saying, had immediately scribbled a prescription for something called Gristle Etouffée at Benny the Spic's Lost Horizon Cafe, to be followed by "hot tub and sturdy colonics."

Hazard shook his head. The dream still haunted him. He thought someday he would learn its true meaning.

He stood up to make ready for horrid night.

At six, DeSky pulled up at the Hazard house in his 1987 blue Lincoln. "Nah, I don't want no limo," the agent had grimaced; "then the driver'll tell us he's real good luck and drove Lucas and Spielberg to the opening of *Star Wars.* They're a pain in the ass, these guys, they're fulla shit. Come on, now, get in or we're gonna be late."

When the car had beetled into the line for drop-off, the scene at the theater was pandemonic. Everywhere strobe lights flashed and blinded while Army Archerd lurked near the curbside interviewing stars for the television camera and cordoned-off fans huzzahed and oohed. Adding to the din and raucous cacaphony, two obscure religious groups waved signs while chanting slogans protesting the film. The Demonics, a Bakersfield cult that worshipped Satan and owned a large chain of health food stores, had charged through their spokesman, Vic DiFazio, that *The Satanist* was "blatantly discriminatory," giving Satan an undeserved press. "So okay, that's just the Devil's thing, alright? Being fucky," DeFazio had vividly asserted sometime earlier. "So why are we getting all bent out of shape?" The other group, Satanists and

Exorcists for Choice, believed strongly that "only the persons possessed" had the right to choose whether to expel their demons.

DeSky took his cigar from his mouth and smiled warmly. "Hey,
that's great. I just love all this shit, don't you?"

The director said, "I think I'm about to throw up."

The agent turned to him. "You serious?"

"Yes." His voice was strained.

"You wanna get out here, kid?"

Hazard nodded and started from the car.

"I'm gonna have me a beer across the street at the Roosevelt,"
drawled DeSky. "Come and get me when it's over. I can't watch
this kind of stuff."

Hazard nodded, slammed the door and threw up in the street.

"Holy shit," the agent murmured. "This thing must be a whole
lot worse than I thought."

Hazard took a handkerchief out, wiped his mouth, then hustled
toward the brightly lit entrance of the theater. His intention was
to slip past Archerd undetected, but he heard his name being
called, turned around and saw the interviewer waving him over.
Hazard paused and then wretchedly trudged to the camera.

"Yes, ladies and gentlemen," Archerd beamed, "the director of
the year's most awaited film, the luminous, distinguished Jason
Hazard himself. Come on, Jason, come in a little closer, if you
would."

Hazard glumly moved in a few steps.

"Well, Jason, this is quite big night for you, isn't it? In fact, it's
a pretty big night for us all. This is surely, and without exaggera-
tion, the most anticipated, talked-about film in a decade. How are
you feeling about it?"

"Okay."

"There was so much secrecy surrounding the film. Is it true it
has a scene that almost got you an X?"

The director felt the stirrings of nausea returning. Staring
wildly and fighting for control, he shook his head.

"No comment? Still keeping things under wraps?"

A quick headshake.

"Can you say there's any truth to the rumors of mysterious

happenings on the set? Bad accidents, unexplained fires and the like?"

The director stared glassily into space. In his eyes tiny points of panic shone.

"That bad," said Archerd, frowning.

A terse, quick nod.

"Arthur Zelig just talked to us, Jason. Was he just being terribly modest when he said he had nothing to do with the picture, that it's been all your baby every step of the way?"

Hazard bolted and ran toward the theater entrance.

Archerd stood watching him expressionlessly, then turned his head and looked into the camera. "Mysterious," he ruminated gravely. "Everything connected with this picture is eerie." He turned to the side as a man in a serape and sombreo approached him. "Let's see now, who's this?" Archerd wondered aloud. "Can you give us your name, sir?"

"No. No names. Djou know you got a really dirty men's room in dis place? Djou people got to try to keep it clean a li'l bedder." He handed the perplexed reporter a card. "Call thees number," he instructed, pointing it out. "Thees lady, she can fine us right away, *no problemo*. Ask for her."

Archerd squinted at the card: " 'Ask for Patsy?' "

Hazard lurched to the theater's immaculate men's room, but by then the spurts of nausea attacking him subsided. He sighed, looked in a mirror, and was shocked by what he saw. *I am looking at a dead man*, he thought, *a fucking corpse*. He grasped the sides of a washbasin, lowered his face and splashed cold water on it, then toweled. He had to go through with this: the contract specified sanctions unless he attended the first public screening. He sighed, combed his hair and walked down to the theater, where the orchestra section was abuzz with excitement, not only because of the novel's notoriety, but the airtight secrecy as well that had cloaked the production from the start, no less than the rumors of weird misfortunes relating to the cast and crew of the film. Sprightly Hazard, for example, was rumored to have given birth to a child with no nose whatsoever and the head of a wasp, a report that, when it reached the comedian George Burns, caused that icon to observe, with a tap at his cigar, "Well, at least it can join any club that it wants."

The director skulked past people who knew him and went to the roped-off last three rows where he sat beside a powerful Hollywood agent. In front of him were Zelig, Miss Peltz and Drood. The mogul turned around to him and stared. Hazard sensed the smile of spite behind the mask. "Hello, Jason. I'm so happy to see you here. Look, Jonathan—it's our brilliant director. You must greet him."

Drood turned around. "Oh, hello, Mr. Hazard."

"Hello."

"Have you read my pages yet, Mr. Hazard?."

"No, I thought I'd wait to see them on the screen tonight."

"Ah, here we go, here we go!" rasped Zelig excitedly. He eagerly turned toward the screen. The lights in the theater were slowly dimming and an ominous tympany sound began throbbing through the speakers of the theater like the beating of a heart. There were gasps, and though the buzzing of the audience softened, the level of excitement in the whispers intensified. The curtains began to rustle back.

"Gee, whiz, here we go, Mr. Zelig," said Drood. "I'm excited. Thanks again for this really neat seat."

"You're the reason we're all here, my dear boy."

"I am?"

The film faded up and after the Zelig Studio logo there appeared on the screen an unusual version of the so-called possessory above-the-title credit. It read:

Completely Jason Hazard's
"THE SATANIST"

Hazard sank lower into his seat and contemplated sneaking out of the theater after placing a dummy in his place.

"Is this seat taken or isn't it empty?" the director heard a vacuous, breathy voice asking. He looked up at a stunning young blonde in her twenties and the source of the heady perfume he was inhaling. "Oh, my God, you're Jason Hazard!" the girl said excitedly, a hand pressed up to her face. "Oh, I'm your biggest, biggest fan! Can I sit here? Is it empty?"

Hazard nodded, looked away and murmured, "Sure."

"I'm Barely Barcelona," said the girl. She sat down. "Oh, this is really too tubular for expression! I mean, I used to be a model but now I'm an actress. And now here I am sitting with my favorite director. Oh God! I mean, I only saw *Illegible* six *times*! Incidentally, are you *sure* this seat is empty?"

"I'm certain."

"I'll be quiet now. I guess you want to concentrate on things? Just remember, though, I really am a very good actress."

With a flip of her hair, she turned her head toward the screen. The title had faded up to eager applause, and then a deadly, awed hush of anticipation had fallen on an audience eager to be thrilled. As the scene in the Georgetown house began, the young actress, while vacantly staring straight ahead, placed her hand high up against Hazard's inner thigh. "Oh, your wife is so beautiful," she whispered. "What an actress."

Startled, Hazard froze, numbly staring at the screen, but when he reached down to pull away the errant hand, the actress clutched at it, squeezing it more tightly than ever. "God, I can't believe I'm sitting here next to you!" she huskily whispered. "Gee, your hand is so cold, it's like ice. Warm heart? Okay, I'm not going to talk anymore."

Hazard tried to extract his hand but found he couldn't; the girl had the grip of a frenzied hawk. He decided to fix his attention to the screen. The scene in the Georgetown house had begun, the telephone call from the assistant director.

"Ooh, this is so scary!" the actress whispered.

Hazard tensed as the dreaded moment approached. But when Sprightly walked into the darkened bedroom and whispered, "I sure do love you, Guy"—this followed by a delicate but definite braying—no more than a nervous little titter broke out among an audience gripped by their expectations and quelled by the director's and the novel's reputation. Some took it for a dream or for a purposely bizarre demonic delusion, while others floated judgment and awaited the certain disclosure of its deeper and true meaning. But when Emory Bunting played his scene with John Tremaine proposing the exorcism of a mule, a thunderclap of laughter burst forth from the audience; then another, and again and again. Hazard's body temperature dropped eighteen degrees and he began to sink lower and lower into his seat, and as the laughter continued unremittingly, Zelig turned around in his seat to stare at him with naked satisfaction.

"The mule has been speaking in an unknown tongue."

"Oh, I daresay he has."

The roof fell in.

Hazard could simply bear no more. Though reluctant to miss the musical sequence, he leaped up and started an escape from the theater just as the scene with the Bishop had ended and a loud and giddy chattering erupted in the audience. He made it to the aisle but his progress was slowed by his need to continually cuff at the starlet who was clinging to his leg with both her arms: in the foyer, the strength of four male ushers was required to pry her grip loose from the director's body even as Hazard continued to cuff her. "I—cannot—*help* you!" he would grit with each slap. "My career is *over!* I can—not *help!*"

They were able to free him somewhere in that golden land between the footsteps of Gary Cooper and the prints of Betty Grable's legs. At the end, as they pried the starlet loose, she asked Hazard, "Am I ever going to see you again?"

The shattered director found DeSky at the Roosevelt.

"Tony!"

"Hey, Jason! Holy shit, kid, who died?"

"I think me. Come on, Tony, drink up. Let's move, let's get out of the neighborhood."

"Uh-oh. No good, huh?"

"They're laughing their asses off!"

"Yeah, you said they might do that. Too bad," said the agent. He knocked back the rest of his vodka neat and set the shot glass down on the bar with a clunk. "Well, at least it's all over." He looked at Hazard's hand. "Hey, they really must hate it," he said. "I can see there where somebody bit you."

The beginning of the drive back to Malibu was somber, except for a brief and unsatisfying moment when the agent had to swerve to avoid a yeti that had just emerged from Barney's Beanery and was lumbering across the street. Momentarily, Hazard was roused from his funk.

"Hey, Tony, did you *see* that?" he blurted excitedly. "Did you see what that was back there?"

"Yeah, I saw him last week," said the agent unflappably. "We had a talk. He's fulla shit just like I thought."

Thereafter, a funereal silence reigned until the car reached the beach at Santa Monica, whereon the agent, perhaps inspired by the shine of the moon upon the waters, began to descant upon his future retirement and how he'd recently purchased twenty acres of sloping land in Malibu Canyon so that one day he could spend all his time raising goats, and then how, when that vivid exploration had ended, he looked forward to the coming of Thanksgiving Day, when, as always, he and Patsy and the children would have dinner at the Roy Rogers Restaurant in Palm Springs. Then he talked about death. "Someone oughta write a book about that," he said raspily. "I mean, think about it: death: what a downer! Somethin's really kocked up about the whole idea."

"Tony, why are you bringing this subject up *now?*"

"I dunno. I just think about it a lot."

The subject arose again at the Hazards', after the agent had come in for a beer. They were sitting in the teahouse, close to the surf on this clear and quiet moonlit night. Hazard had come in to find a note from Sprightly: "Hope you're okay," she had written.

"Don't wake me, I took two sleeping pills and told the service to hold all our calls. I set the alarm for 7:15. Make sure you're not up too late tonight, pie, and leave the door unlocked for Ralph, I think he's out walking on the beach with that Pakistani jerk who bought Joey's Ribs. You're the greatest director in this world and I love you more than anything."

She'd signed it with kisses.

Hazard poured a shot of tequila for himself in the hope that it would punch out his lights fairly soon, got the agent a beer, and then aimlessly chatted: about the business, Hazard's future, what film he'd make first. Then, as more alcohol was consumed, the agent brought the conversation back to death. "I had a brother with terminal cancer," he recounted in that beery, laryngeal voice. "Near the end I had him over at Lipschitz Memorial; you know the one, I can't think, I've got a block. I'd made a deal with the doc he should feel no pain, so they had him juiced up on cloud nine all the time. So one day I walk in and he doesn't see me, he's lookin' straight ahead like he's concentrating hard, like he's listening to someone at the foot of the bed, and then he nods and he says to this nobody standing there, 'So, okay, so what happens after that?' Then the nurse comes in and interrupts. Later on while I'm with him, he starts in talkin' to himself pretty good. Yeah, he's lookin' out the window, ya see, and he's smilin' and he says, 'I finally understand it. I finally know the whole purpose of life.' Then he shakes his head and looks down and starts laughin'. 'It's so simple,' he says, 'so simple,' and he's chucklin' so hard he's got to wipe at his eyes. Another nurse came in right then and made me leave, she had to take some blood or somethin' from him, so I never got to hear from my brother his secret. That same night he died. Death. What a fuckin' disgrace. We gotta do somethin', Jace, we gotta stop it, we gotta throw a fund-raisin' dinner or somethin', maybe somethin' at the Hollywood Bowl with Frank. Anyway, the thing I wanna ask you, Jason, is you think he coulda really been talkin' to someone?"

"Who?"

"My brother."

"You mean talking to spirits?"

"Yeah, spirits."

"No."

"I didn't want you to say that, Jason."

"When you're dead you're dead."

"That right?"

"That's right."

"Who negotiated that deal?"

After midnight, Ralph filtered in off the beach, took one look at the faces of Hazard and DeSky and decided not to ask about the fortunes of the film. He turned and walked back to his room and went to bed. A little after one, the agent left with a hug and a promise to return Hazard's phone calls promptly. The director poured one more drink, a large glass filled with Bristol Cream sherry, then sat with it gloomily staring at the ocean in the hope that some voice there would say, "You did right," and by the last boozy sip, by the final regret, he had once again fallen asleep in his chair.

He dreamed that Ralph was dating Madonna.

Tap tap.

The director creaked open his eyes. Dawn was seeping in and DeSky was at the window, tapping at the glass with an index finger. Hazard gave a muffled little grunt, got up, shuffled to the door, pulled it open, said, "Shit," and then turned and slumped back toward his nest in despond. "Hey, Tony, what's up?" he groggily uttered. He saw a small object on the seat of his chair. Unthinkingly, he picked it up, clasped it in his hand, plopped down in the chair and shielded his eyes against the bright stabs of the rising sun.

"Okay, now, just listen to this," slurred DeSky, padding in with a raincoat worn over pajamas. "Here's the good news: my Mexican cleaners gave notice. Last night they called Patsy and said they saw the picture and they couldn't be connected with that kind of filth."

"What's the bad news?"

"It looks like you're employable again."

The film was closing in on the final fade when the agent turned around in his seat to speak to Zelig. "This is big, Arthur. Huge.

Bigger than Ghost. *It's got to do three hundred million easy. Whose idea was it to make it as a comedy? Hazard's?"*

The end-title music was swelling. Credits crawled. The agent turned back to join the spirited applause. Zelig was bewildered, at first, in shock, then he felt a great anger and wrenching dismay, but as he heard the applause sustaining, growing louder, the wild shouts of "Bravo!" now lacing the air, he abruptly gaped and froze all motion.

"My God, I can see!" he gasped. "I can see!"

The crowd rose to its feet. The applause was thunderous.

"Down in front!" Zelig shouted at first, but when he stood and peered up at the screen he grew livid.

"Where's my credit?" he squealed. "I don't see my credit!"

The excited applause and acclaim continued. Distraught, Zelig started now to shout at the screen: "I picked the director! I shaped the script! I picked the heads of department and the cast and the crew! I heard the rushes! WHERE'S MY CREDIT?"

The litany of "Where's my credit?" continued long after there was no one in the theater left to hear it. Getting into his limo an hour later, the mogul said tightly, "You'll pay for this, Jeff."

"Isn't this somethin'?" mused DeSky. He slapped at an L.A. *Times* review with its references to "catharsis" and a "cleansing of terror." "Same with all of them. I called all around, our guys here and our guys in New York. This goddamn picture of yours is a *smash!* Isn't that what I told you that day at the Plaza?"

"Yeah, Tony. I guess that's why you get the big bucks."

Hazard unclasped his hand just then, and he looked at the object he'd found on his chair. It was a silvery emblem in the form of a female breast intertwined with the block letter "N."

CHAPTER THREE

INTERIM FINAL REPORT

SUBJECT: *Jason Hazard*
DATE: *Friday, December 11*

IN THIS SEASON OF renewal—for some—it is fitting that this difficult case has now closed, although nothing conclusively eviden-
tial has occurred that would alter my steadfast opinion that the
subject, down deep, remains a turd of almost intergalactic
standing. In the meantime, for the moment I count my bless-
ings.

Upon Mr. Hazard's return to New York, he was, as he ex-
pressed it, once again "hot." His plan was to seclude himself
for a time in his Connecticut weekend house until he'd finished what he planned to embark upon next, a sweeping epic
that he planned to shoot entirely in Egypt and provisionally
entitled *Even* Farther *Out of Africa*. It was at this time, however, beginning with his learning that his wife was pregnant,
that the subject's neurotic symptoms first appeared, along with
a chronic and nightly repetition of his earlier bizarre, lucid
dream of exorcism. In this dream, the subject's unconscious—
so much wiser and possessing greater knowledge than the conscious—signaled him correctly that the key to his ultimate

well-being lay in centering his cares outside of himself, while the various exorcists in the dream represented the subject's resistance to this fact. The onset of neurosis was in part a delaying tactic as the subject struggled to decide whether or not to devote the next year to his family or proceed with his long-cherished project in Egypt; and was also partly a terrified response to the prospect of sharing his wife with a sibling. Adding further to the subject's disorientation was a cynism bred of the positive critical and public response to the *Satanist* film, with deepest meanings being fashioned and plucked from its inanities, thus intensifying festering doubts in his mind about the glowing critical evaluations of most of his previous body of work. All of this, admittedly, is to the good.

The situation as it stands at this present moment is that Hazard, who has gone from "hot" to "sizzling"—the film, he says, has grossed $250 million, although, curiously, the producer states it *"lost* fifty million"—has turned down all offers, including his Egyptian epic, and decided to teach a course in film at Columbia University for at least the next two years, thus "giving back," as he so nauseously expresses it, and "just being famous for a while." After that, his options, he says, are open, but adds that if indeed he returns to making films, it will be with what he speaks of as a "new sensibility," by which he means, I would reasonably presume, that he intends to stop fondling himself in public.

In the meantime, of course, it is crucial to recognize that he has taken but a hesitant step; the "old" man still lurks underneath the "new," and a relapse could easily occur in the future, possibly as early as New Year's Day. But I am sanguine.

I cannot take credit for the change in this man, nor can any form of *deus ex machina*, either, by which I mean the silvery emblem that he "found," yet another of this patient's preposterous delusions (or, perhaps, an infuriating effort to vex me: I have had its atomic structure analyzed and it is made of terrestrial metals); Hazard's reformation occurred, he tells me, when he heard the first cry of his newborn son. The head is not enough to make sense of our affairs, it seems; we cannot underestimate the heart.

Part Eight

EPILOGUE

A LETTER FROM
AN UNKNOWN FRIEND

Dear Mr. Hazard,

I hope you'll forgive this intrusion on your time. You don't know me, but I've long been your great admirer. I've seen every one of your films and love them all, most especially your most recent, the exciting *The Satanist*. When I saw it, a disturbing thing happened to me, which is why I am writing this letter. Call it a dream, if you prefer, but in fact it was a chilling and powerful vision. At this point I must explain to you that I am a psychic very much in the mold of Laura Mars (Do you remember? *The Eyes of Laura Mars?*), and if what I experienced has any validity—and no one but you can tell me that—then I must warn you that I feel you are in terrible danger. In brief, I had a vision you were under treatment due to a severe delusional state that reduced you to the status of a dangerous psychopath: you heard voices in the ocean call your name; attempted to exorcise your cat; had discourse with interplanetary abductees; suspected Barbra Streisand and Julie Andrews of criminally breaking into your home; had attacks of phaneromania, phantasmophobia, acute bruxism and DeMille-ophobia; and have been praised for directing a film that in fact you did not direct at all inasmuch as almost all of the creative choices were actually made by some person named Zelig. (Who is he? I didn't see his name in the credits.)

Anyway, I saw this awful danger was lurking, the chance that you—what was that line in my vision?—might go back to "running around inside the squirrel cage of your ego." A frightening figure in my vision said to warn you never to go back to making films. It said that if you did, you would probably die. I won't mention what else he had to say about your films, or the names of all the people who would put you to death. Does any of this make any sense, Mr. Hazard? Or was it just a crazy, lucid dream that I had?

Turning to another subject entirely, I wonder if you're aware of how psychics have to struggle just to make ends meet, especially here along Central Park West where the rents are exorbitantly high. I refuse to take money for any of my work; it's a gift, and to use it for profit would be wrong. Under these circumstances, however, I thought that perhaps I could accept a contribution, inasmuch as if any of these matters came to light they could prove quite embarrassing for you, I think, and, much more importantly, it would probably make it impossible for you to secure a Completion Bond. Don't directors need to have one of these before they can make a film?

Could you arrange to gather fifty thousand dollars in cash by December 21st? I urge you to do so. Place it in a soft-leather Gucci bag, and on that morning I will call and instruct you as to where and when you are to deposit it. One heartfelt word of warning: time and punctuality will be of the essence—there's an auction at Sotheby's the following day that I simply cannot afford to miss: They are offering a garter belt found among the personal effects of Sigmund Freud. *Do not cross me, you maniac, or you're meat!*

Yours until the stars lose their shine,

A Friend